To the Pastures

By: Lucy Girolamo

Lucygirolamo.com

Published by: **Sunlitheart Publishing**

This book is dedicated to all Cubans.
Those that were political prisoners and those who gave
their lives in the pursuit of liberty.

Printed in the United States of America

Published by: **SunlitHeart Publishing, L.L.C.**
Website: Lebiachatman.com, **Instagram:** Sunlitheart Publishing

Edited by: Karie Athens

ISBN: 978-0-578-64647-3

Acknowledgments

To my parents, Jose and Lucia. Who sacrificed everything and worked tirelessly to provide their daughters with a better life in a free country. Their love, nurturing, and teaching were the foundation for my success and the inspiration for my fight for civil justice.

To my sisters, Monica and Ana, who joined me during the journey as I learned to embrace the United States.

To my nieces and nephews, Camilla, who illustrated the map, Gavin, Tessa, Rose, Madeline, Jake, Gwendolyn, Evelyn, Emmanuel, Mateus, and Mia for their inquisitive minds.

To my publisher, Lebia Chatman, for taking a chance and helping me keep my promise to my dad by bringing this dream to fruition.

To my numerous family and friends for their support. My aunt and uncle, Isabel and Vicente, for their love and aid, when we arrived in the United States. José F. Lamas, for his knowledge and advice. Lisa Thill-Molitor, for inspiring me to reach higher. My Writers Group, Laura Kania, and my editor, Karie Athens, for their insights and guidance.

Most importantly, to my husband, John, and my children, Kayla, Cristian, and Samuel, who motivated, supported, and encouraged me through this endeavor. Their curiosity and quest for their heritage was the inspiration for this book.

The following page contains a map of the locations that are frequently referenced throughout this book.

6

1-Concrete Walls

1963

Cristian walks through the coffee finca, or plantation, searching for ripening plants. It's a cool morning on the finca, and the lush coffee trees offer pleasant shade. He enjoys tending the plants early before the sizzling, humid, summer heat sets in. The saltwater breeze filling the air refreshes and soothes his lungs as he looks up to see Trogons chirp and flutter on the piñón trees nearby.

The finca dominates a hilltop in the small Cuban town of Imias. Cristian looks down to admire his family home, a peach painted ranch home sheltered from the sun by a Spanish tile roof. The backyard hums with animals grazing safely within the post and rail fence. He daydreams that someday he will take over his family's prosperous business and continue the legacy his father worked so hard to build.

"Cristian!" a name calls from the distance, interrupting his pleasant daydream.

The familiar voice sends his heart racing. He has been waiting for her and dashes down the hill to meet her. They head to one of his favorite places, looking forward to feeling the turquoise sea flowing between their toes. Ahead they spot where the beach meets the hillside, guarded by giant boulders. Majestic waves roar as they crash against the stones. Behind the shelter of rocks, they settle down for a peaceful picnic on the white sand. Grinning, he looks up at the brilliant blue sky.

"*Bong, bong, bong,*" the prison's bell blares loudly.

Waking up, blinking slowly, he sees his surroundings. Cristian's grin turns to a frown and a pit settles in his stomach as he comes to the painful realization that it was all a dream. It is time to begin the monotonous routine of the past six years. He climbs down from the top bunk, staggering, groggily to the sink. He drips a few drops of stale, tawny water on his palm, to wipe his face, and rinses out his mouth, then plods back to make his bed, checking his work for perfection. The dream sneaks back into memory. *How he desperately longs to dig his toes into soft white sand.* He pauses to digest his surroundings: the voices around him, the claustrophobic concrete walls, and the suffocating air he breathes in daily. Every morning he has the same reminders of bloodshed and a war he fought but ultimately… lost.

"Line up!" the guard yells, making the second wake up call.

Cristian steps out of his cell to scan the hall. He spots two men, and they exchange discreet nods. Inmates stand cemented outside their cells waiting for their orders. The row of men starts its walk to the dining room, trudging along the corridor in single file. When they arrive, he notices a familiar face from back home. He starts to reflect back to when his life changed for the sake of freedom.

2 – Honradez

By 1952, Cuba's corrupt leaders had managed to fill their pocketbooks as labor union conflicts arose, and poverty increased. On March 10, 1952, Fulgencio Batista led a coup and took power. Under his control, economic problems continued for the Cuban people. The Mafia moved in, growing their empire. They flooded the island with glamorous casinos, high-end hotels and elegant nightclubs. Batista's bank accounts flourished as gang violence and gambling increased. His henchmen kept order as their wallets also gained weight.

Small-secluded country towns were less affected by the politics and economic problems. In the small town of Imias, politicians seldom came around. Any who did, respected the patriarch of the prominent family in town. The family's status shielded the town from the growing tension on the island, but not for long.

1957

Cristian, the fifth of eight children in the Enriquez family, wakes up to the first chirps of Cuban bullfinches outside his window. Stumbling out of bed, Cristian, a tall figure, yanks on his gray work pants. He fits his guayabera over his tan muscles, carved through hours of hard work beside his siblings. Slowly, he swings open the curtain that separates his room from the rest of the house; he tiptoes through the ranch home to avoid disturbing the rest of the family.

He cannot wait to step out into the fresh air; a gentle wind sweeps by and he inhales the sea breeze. The scent of the Caribbean saltwater refreshes his lungs. Down the street, a neighbor sets up the tables and chairs at his café, as the town begins to come alive. Cristian strides onto the calm gravel road, then jumps into the family truck for the trip to one of their two cattle ranches. His house sits near the northern edge on the only road in town, referred to as la línea by locals, which cuts through the middle of Imías.

The sun peeks out. The melodies of a giant kingbird and a Cuban gnatcatcher fill his ears. It is a tranquil drive on the gravel road. On the south side, tall, lush, banana, and Caribbean pine trees dwell alongside orchids and Barbados lilies. The north side of the road offers a glorious view of the rolling green finca hills, as the majestic mountains drape the background.

During his serene drive on the roadway, he daydreams of the bright blue Ford convertible that he hopes to own someday. It is magnificent; a full-size four-door sedan, powered by a V8. He imagines the feel of the smooth tan leather seat, his right hand gripping the polished vanilla steering wheel. With the white top down, the wind combs through his thick black hair. His favorite song comes on the radio to snap him out of the dream. He begins to sing as he rolls up to a local campesino, a farmer leading his horse. While politely waving, he spots his destination up ahead.

He pulls up to the barn that sits next to the main house on the ranch. The truck comes to a stop by the barn entrance; his footsteps on the gravel drive alert the horses grazing behind the split-rail fence. He gives the wooden door a shove and with quick, sure steps heads to the back of the building. Hustling through the barn, he smells fresh hay in an empty stable, a sign they were tending to a sick animal. The adjacent stable has branding tools in preparation for new livestock. He hurries to the milking stable, where a cow looks up at him, munching her morning meal. Behind her, an employee fills a bucket with her milk.

"Good morning," the man salutes Cristian. "Welcome home! We've missed you."

"Good morning. It's good to be back," he responds, picking up a bucket filled with milk then pouring it in an empty canister. Cristian sits on a stool next to another cow and begins to milk it, while they catch up.

"Is this the last one?" Cristian observes, lifting the bucket he just filled.

"Yes, you can start loading the full canisters in the corner," the employee says turning his head to point to their location.

Cristian loads the milk in the back of the truck to transport them to the family store, the Honradez. Papa named the store to memorialize Cristian's grandfather, who taught his family honor.

The sun now sits on the horizon as the ranch cattle graze. Cristian piles the last of the milk canisters heading back down the country road, where a picturesque landscape of fincas surrounds him. He admires the horses and mules in the distance, as they graze on his family's lands. His route takes him past the family's mango orchards. They flourish in rows of rich vegetation that stretch for miles. On a nearby hill resides the family's bountiful coffee finca.

As he pulls up to the store, he spots Papa and Samuel, his youngest brother, setting up the merchandise. Samuel, a muscular man with thick hair and a light mustache, usually works shifts with him. He comes out to help Cristian unload the milk, carrying the containers to the refrigerator at the back of the store. Papa, a tall, slender, gray-haired man, continues to organize the rest of the food items on shelves and hangs apparel on racks.

At the Honradez, the family's primary business and source of income, customers buy food, clothing, liquor, medicine, and auto parts. Papa owns thriving supermarkets in Pozanco, San Ignacio, Veguita and San Antonio. He transports the harvested crops and milk from their land in Imias to these locations.

Two customers stroll in to gossip with Papa. Walking through the store, Cristian hears a casino announcement on the radio.

The customers vent after hearing the broadcast.

"Those casinos are going to be nothing but trouble!" one announces.

"I hear that things aren't that great in the capital," the second man says. "Cubans are dissatisfied with Batista! They say people are rebelling."

"Of course, they are rebelling. Batista's corruption is running rampant! He's getting a lot of money from the Mafia and profiting from their businesses," he fumes looking at Papa.

"And beware if you oppose him!" The second man slams his hand on the counter. "My brother lives in

Havana. He was walking home when he saw a swarm of turkey vultures in the distance. As he got closer, he noticed something hanging from a tree. Then he saw a group of people."

"What was it?" the other man inquires.

"The most gruesome sight he has ever seen! A young man was hanging! Bruised, bloody, and nails missing. His mother laid on the ground crying in agony, while the others were trying to get his body down."

"You're making that up!" Papa snaps defensively.

"I swear on the Holy Bible! My brother wouldn't make that up."

"I read in the paper that unemployment rates are rising, especially among college graduates," the other man says. "Is that what's fueling the student riots and protest in the universities?" he inquires, looking at the boys.

"Those are all rumors," Papa casually says, taking the attention away from his boys. "We have nothing to worry about. Everything will work itself out."

Papa tries to avoid discussing their education, a sore topic with the boys. Forced to discontinue their studies, Cristian and his brothers have decided to move back home for a while. A truck transported all their belongings from Havana back home, where politicians respect and hold

Papa in high regard. They hope things get back to normal. Then they can return to their studies.

"Hurry up and get some breakfast," Papa commands Cristian. "Your brother and I already ate. Take a canister of milk with you."

"Ok, I'll return shortly," he politely responds.

Cristian carries a milk canister, marching through the store to the door that connects to their house. Most businesses in the country towns of Cuba are attached to the owners' homes.

He opens the door, detecting the scraping of a pan and silverware on plates in the kitchen, proceeding through the house his stomach grumbles as he spots breakfast set on the dining table. With care, he places the canister on the kitchen counter for Mama.

"Here's our milk." He gives her a gentle kiss on the cheek.

"Thank you!" she smiles. "Go eat."

Famished, he quickly gobbles up the meal to get ready for another day of full labor.

3 – Imias

Batista's corruption rises, as he becomes allies with the Mafia and profits from their casinos, hotels, and nightclubs. Cubans are alarmed as the gap between the rich and the poor increases. Batista instills fear in those that oppose him. Protesters vanish, while others are gun down or beaten, and the mutilated cadavers are left hanging beside public roads.

1957

Later that evening, Mama, a short, slender, brunette, finishes cleaning up in the kitchen after dinner. Papa is reading the paper, his usual nightly routine before he heads to bed. Everyone else is down for the night. She walks into the dining room to kiss Papa on the forehead as she heads to bed. He finishes his last page and turns in for the night. The lights go off in the house when Papa settles down for a peaceful night's sleep. As he dozes off, he reflects on the chaos all over the island, grateful to have everyone safe and sound back home.

At 1:00 am, a loud blast shakes the house causing everyone to jump out of bed. Gunshots cut through the silence of the night. They hear wailing echoing outside.

"What's that?" Samuel shouts.

"What's happening?" one of the children cries.

Panic and screams fill the atmosphere. Adults yank hollering children out of bed, and a stampede of bodies runs into the dining room. "Everyone get down!" Papa demands.

Cristian peeks out the back window to see gunshots flashing across the field, while dirt scatters in a fiery blaze. Samuel goes to the front of the house to peek out of the window. Down the street, he sees the blast of a bomb light up the sky, as debris flies through the air. The smoke dissipates, exposing burning fragments drifting to the ground.

"They're fighting across the field!" Cristian hollers.

"I see blasts at the end of the street by the guard headquarters!" Samuel shouts.

Rebels move into Imias to hide in the mountains. While the town slept, they made their move to attack the police station, down the street from the Enriquez house. Gunshots ricochet at the edge of town and in the hills. Flaring rubble sprays in the air, as a veil of smoke floods the hillside. Shrapnel rains when blasts from bombs roll down the street, making shutters shake and doors quake.

Cristian squats next to Mama, trying not to let her feel his heart palpitations. Everyone lies low, away from the windows. The house trembles as constant gunshots and bombings continue, while adults cover and cuddle the screaming children to console them. For the next several hours, through the shots and bombs, everyone falls in and out of sleep.

Deep in the night, the fighting stops, and they manage to get a couple of hours of sleep before waking up to start their day. Weeping children cling to adults as everyone cautiously begins to make their way through the house.

Papa scouts the house, afraid that bullets made their way in. Anxiety consumes him as he imagines bullet holes in the walls and broken furniture. Then announces, "Everything's fine inside," he reassures everyone.

Mama and the girls get breakfast ready. The boys make their way outside to check the rest of the property.

"Everything's clear out here," Cristian shouts.

"There's no damage to the property, but everyone's pretty scared," Papa frowns as he talks to Mama.

Locals wake up and cautiously step out. A man waves his arms fiercely, yelling at his demolished front door as his wife kneels on the gravel weeping. Men and women clean up chunks of concrete and wood posts on the street and sidewalk. The Enriquez boys dash around helping their neighbors tidy the town. Thankfully, the turmoil in the night had not penetrated their peaceful city. Despite the current serenity, Papa worries about the family's safety. Unsure of the duration of this battle, Papa decides to relocate the family temporarily. Papa's successful businesses throughout the island allow the family flexibility to seek shelter in a house they own in nearby San Ignacio. Worried that their home might incur damages during this turbulent time, they pack up essential belongings.

"Papa, we'll put up sandbags and barricade the windows and doors," Cristian states.

"Yes, we'll be fine if we stay. Plenty of men here to take care of everyone," Samuel adds.

"Absolutely not!" Papa responds. "I will not put my family in harm's way. Pack up!"

4 – Beans

July 26, 1953, a Cuban rebel named Fidel Castro opposes Batista's form of government planning an uprising. With a group of rebels, Fidel attacks the Moncada Bastille military barracks in Santiago de Cuba. Batista captures him, but unlike others who oppose the government and led to a gruesome fate; Batista spares Fidel from assassination. He is sentenced and eventually set free.

1957

Early the next morning, the men leave their temporary home in San Ignacio, heading to harvest the coffee in the family's finca. The minibus they use for shuttling the family and employees to satellite locations, now manages their commute to Imias.

Papa, Samuel, and Cristian stop at the house to inspect it. An eerie silence saturates the air. Cristian frowns at the abandoned kitchen as he spots Samuel scanning the bedrooms with clenched fists. Papa eases the tension with directions. "Everything is fine! I'll open the store. You boys get to work."

The brothers stride to the backyard to untie the mules. Patiently they guide the animals through the yard and begin their hike to the coffee finca.

"There's a lot of unrest on the island," Samuel ponders. "We have to do something!"

"People are beginning to revolt against Batista," says Cristian as they begin their trek to the finca. "Everyone's outraged after he ordered the assassination of the university students."

"We can't sit back and allow Batista to get away with murder!" Samuel fumes.

"It's dangerous out there!" Cristian tries to reason. "Batista closed the universities and ordered his guards to take students into custody for questioning. He claims the deaths were terrorist acts."

"You know Batista had those students killed. He's the terrorist!"

"Regardless, we need to lay low. I'm furious too. He's keeping us from getting an education, but things will work out."

They make their climb through lush pastures and are greeted at the top by their family's finca of cocoa trees. Tall, slender yet sturdy trunks prop up bright orange pods canopied by lush leaves. The men lead the mules through the rows of trees to a small clearing. Large arrowhead-shaped leaves of the malanga plant carpet the ground leading to the coffee plants.

Past the foliage, rows of five-foot-tall coffee plants salute them. Dense trees conceal the cherry-covered branches. This is one of Cristian's treasured locations on the family's land, where the fragrance of fresh vegetation, excites his senses. Hypnotized by the tot-tot-tot sound of the toby and rainbow of butterflies whisking through the air, the abundance of life on the hills mesmerizes him.

At their destination, knocking sounds of cuckoos hiding in the bordering shortleaf fig trees, greet the men. The coffee fields bloom with red coffee cherries, which employees diligently pick by hand, while at the edge of the rows, employees stack harvested beans into sacks. Cristian and a muscular employee, who shades his head from the sun with a sombrero, lead the disciplined mules to the processing plant where they unload the sacks to haul them to the fermenting station.

Out of breath, Samuel comes running into the secadero, the coffee drying house. "What do you need?" he asks Cristian.

"Start bringing in the sacks," he directs Samuel.

An employee tends to a section of the secadero, filling giant white tubs with water. The temperature rises quickly in this small structure, which helps the water reach 90 degrees; the perfect environment to ferment coffee beans.

"Start loading the tubs," an employee announces.

"Samuel!" Cristian hollers. "Get over here and help me."

The brothers and men begin depositing beans in the tubs. Diligently the men work on filling all the containers with beans, cautious not to splash too much water. Stacks of empty sacks pile up against the wall. The end of their workday approaches as men splash mops around, soaking up any remaining water. Empty sacks pile on the mules for reuse. A sanitary secadero signals the end of a hard day's work, then the lights go out and Cristian locks up the facility.

The next morning, a kapok tree vibrates with motion as a hutia peaks out of her den. Scouting and sniffing around, she discovers the cause of the commotion and crawls back in the tree. Nearby, Cristian, Samuel, and the crew return to gather the beans to run them through the processing machine. Men pack the processed coffee beans into sacks. Mules quietly graze outside, waiting for their next assignment, as an employee starts stacking the sacks on them. The brothers lead the loaded mules with sacks of processed beans down the hill to the family's warehouse.

"Papa, we have another load," Cristian reports.

"Thank you, boys, good work!" Papa announces. "You got here just in time. Get them into storage fast." A grin surfaces as he proudly watches the hardworking young men he has raised.

As the men pile bags of coffee beans on the shelves, a fall storm rolls in with a downpour to cool off the sweltering ground. Majestic royal palms refresh as they guzzle the rain. On the hills, this seasonal rainfall keeps the land and vegetation of the fincas thriving. In the mountains, rebels seek shelter from the storm underneath the canopy of the trees, waiting for nightfall to make their descent.

As night sets, the men board the company minibus and leave Imias to join the rest of the family in San Ignacio. Mama sets dinner as the family claims their seats around the table.

Back in Imias the town shifts back into a war zone. Batista's fully armed guards come out of hibernation, roaming the streets, forcing the locals to remain indoors. Sandbags surround houses and businesses for additional protection, as rebels lurking in the mountains rain down from the hills to attack the police station and take weapons. Gunshots blaze in the outskirts of town. Screams of injured men echo through the night. Window shutters used to shelter from storms now mute war blasts. Civilians try resting amongst the chaos. Their lives have become a nightmare.

5 – Beach House

In Havana's shipyard, a group of men dressed in chic polo shirts and pants gathers at a loading dock. They puff their cigarettes while masking their eyes behind sunglasses. Meyer Lansky and Lucky Luciano have sent their henchmen to delegate the pickup of their drug shipments. Other mob minions stand guard outside a storage building, with concealed guns underneath their designer suits, securing the smuggled gold and diamonds.

1957

A month passes, while the family settles into their temporary lifestyle, as Papa anticipates the battle will end soon. The women stay in San Ignacio while the men adjust to the long commute for work in Imias. Papa's gas stations become an added convenience to fuel their vehicles for the increased travel.

This evening, after a long day's work, the family feasts on their evening meal of rice, plantains, and picadillo or ground beef. After his dinner, Cristian treks to the yard to occupy himself in chores when a commotion interrupts him. A shadow catches his eye, and he cautiously proceeds to investigate. As he leans over the fence, he spots a tall figure camouflaged in dark clothing, lurking around. Behind that man, he spots another squatting next to a tree.

He dashes towards the house. "Samuel, get out here fast," he yells. Samuel hustles outside, and they sprint to the fence. "Look," Cristian gestures toward the tree. "Are those rebels?" The tall figure waves his wrist several times, waving others over.

"Yeah, hurry, we have to tell Papa," Samuel believes he recognizes one of the men as his rebel friend. He remembers, a few months back in Havana, his friend waved his wrist, in the same manner, to call Samuel over to join him. Samuel imagines climbing the fence to join his fellow Cubans. The conflict within weighs on him. He has contemplated joining the rebels to fight for his right to get the university education he has longed for, but knows Papa will not allow any of his sons to get involved.

Cristian and Samuel scurry into the house, dragging Papa to a bedroom.

"I've heard murmurs of rebels hoping to deplete the government's resources to force Batista out," Papa recalls.

"My friends told me rebels are secretly recruiting," Cristian whispers.

"Our neighbors and other supporters have given the rebels additional weapons," Papa adds.

"The armory in this town is vulnerable to attacks," Samuel reminds them. "I'm sure people have informed the rebels. That could be why they're here now."

"Many Cubans have joined the cause to overthrow Batista, despite the danger. I want you boys to stay out of it!" Papa stresses once again. Worried about his family's safety, he gathers the adults in the dining room to inform them of the sighting. The battle has followed them. Papa decides to abandon this home too, fearing his family will get caught in the crossfire. He heads to the backyard in solitude. With a deep breath, he looks up at the night sky, debating if they should leave. The thought of a family member injured or worse brings tears to his eyes. He clears his throat and heads inside to pack.

When day breaks, preparations begin for a new shelter in their hometown. The women and children gather to repack their belongings in San Ignacio.

Back in Imias, Papa works with an employee at the Honradez as it fills with customers. The Enriquez brothers and a couple of employees gather supplies from their warehouse. The men pack the green bed of the Ford pickup with wood, nails, and tools. The truck pulls away from the warehouse, pressing down la línea. It vibrates with the usual traffic of cars and pedestrians as the men salute the locals on their trek. The cafés, restaurants, and bars buzz with clientele, ignoring the sandbags guarding buildings. Rebels do not venture out of the mountains, and the military conceals themselves in their fort until nightfall. Throughout the day, the stir of laughter and casual conversations fill every establishment as these islanders feverishly work in their businesses.

La línea heads east on this cliff town at the southern coast of Cuba, its edge guarded by a forest of lush tropical evergreen trees and West Indies cherry trees. Royal Poincianas accompanied by spotted laurels with their green and blemished yellow leaves cover the ground. A bouquet of bright lilac Bougainvilleas, yellow bells, and fragrant white butterfly jasmines flowers flourish everywhere. The road veers south as it reaches the beach.

As the vehicle comes to a halt, men climb over the wood panels of the truck's bed at the edge of the beach. At their destination, Cristian takes in the pristine and tranquil surroundings of waves lapping against the shoreline before helping to unload the cargo area. Construction on their simple refuge begins immediately on the beach, a less traveled area. Papa's old fishing boat, generally used for transporting coffee and bananas to their satellite locations, temporarily carries additional building supplies.

The family stays on the beach during the two days of construction. At the west end of the coastline, the cliff of white eroded rocks, capped by overgrown vegetation, barricades the shore from the town. On the sand, a simple shack with two roomy dormitories, a spacious living area, covered by a thatch roof and an outhouse will shelter the family and two employees. This secluded location now becomes their new home.

On their last day of construction, as night sets, Samuel and Cristian are wrestling, laughing and playing at the beach. They take a break, lying on the sand. A glance at the breathtaking country night sky pauses their game. The brilliant Milky Way puts on a spectacular show of a million twinkling luminous bodies as they stay up late for their habitual long talks.

"You know we can't sit back and do nothing," Samuel is beginning to grow restless and wants to help the rebel cause.

"What are you talking about?" sitting up, Cristian asks feeling confused.

"We have so many friends out there fighting to get our country back. We have to help." Samuel sits up and states desperately.

"If we get caught up in this, Papa will be furious. Besides, it's dangerous!"

"You have never backed away from a fight. You're always beating up guys that mess with Victor. This bastard is messing with our country, our education, and the future. We need to kick his ass!" Samuel explodes.

"This is not a fight with bullies on the street. It's life or death. You know what Batista's men do if they catch you, don't you!"

"Yeah, I've heard of the tortures."

"Yeah, you've heard! It's not just a slap on the wrist. Rebels report that their comrades are burned with cigarettes, choked with wrenches, slashed, and strangled with a cable! If they're lucky, they're spared torture and assassinated," Cristian barks, grabbing Samuel by the shoulders and shaking him. "This is not a street fight."

"Cristian, we have to do something. We can't sit back and watch all our friends fight. That's not like us. Papa has busted his ass to create this enterprise. Our town flourishes, thanks to all his sweat and tears."

"We are safe down here. Politicians around here respect Papa and don't bother us."

"How long do you think it will take Batista to want a piece of Papa's business? That greedy bastard will come here. It's just a matter of time."

"I don't know, it's too dangerous," Cristian tries to reason with his brother.

"I've made up my mind! You can join me if you want, brother. If you don't, I understand."

Samuel pats Cristian on the back as he gets up. He hoped Cristian would join him as he did in all his other endeavors. Suddenly he feels alone, but this is something he must do.

Cristian picks up a small rock in the sand. He grips it tight in his hand, brooding over his conversation with Samuel. *What can he say to make Samuel change his mind*, he thinks to himself. Realizing his stubborn brother will not change his mind, he thrusts the rock in the water.

In the days that follow, Samuel sneaks away from time to time to secretly assist rebels.

"I'm going to check on the mules," Samuel tells Cristian. His code for slipping away.

"Be careful!" Cristian shouts, looking around to see if anyone is looking. A pit sits at the bottom of his stomach, and he begins to work to distract himself.

Samuel creeps between shrubs and ducks underneath fallen trees, looking back every few seconds to make sure no one is behind him. His heart stops when he sees a shadow behind a tree. He drops to the ground and thinks about Cristian's last words. *Should he have listened to his brother and stayed out of this fight?* A plump pig comes out of the shadow, and with a sigh of relief, he gets up and continues to his destination.

6 – Fisherman

*Batista steals funds assigned to public health,
education, and maintenance. The multi-millionaire assigns
his military to protect the Mafia. Censorship of radio
stations and publications tightens. The riches of the
government do not reach the working Cuban. Anyone who
opposes the government will be tortured or face death.*

1957

Weeks went by, Imias becomes a ghost town.
Locals flee their beloved city in the evenings for safety.
The fighting in the mountains and hills has spilled into the
city and street. At the beach shelter, the sea waves no
longer block out the roars of gunfire in town. Accustomed
to the bombings and gunshots, the family is comforted with
the knowledge that the battle remains contained in the city.

One evening, Cristian and Samuel sit on the beach
by the mouth of the river. Cristian has a hand full of sea
grapes he gathered from the bushes nearby. Samuel draws
figures in the sand with a stick.

"Right there, 11 o'clock is the Big Dipper," Cristian
points to the sky.

"Yeah, I see it," Samuel responds. "Show me another."

Suddenly, voices distract Cristian. "What was that?"

"Sounds like rebels."

"Should we tell Papa?"

"Don't worry about them. They won't do anything. They're just checking things out."

"How do you know that?"

"I just do!"

The next morning, the family wakes up to the usual routine. Mama prepares breakfast. The men enjoy their toast, eggs, and sip on their café. After breakfast, the men pile up in the vehicles. Half go to the fincas and the rest to the Honradez.

At the Honradez, Cristian and Samuel help Papa stock the shelves.

"I went for a walk last night along the beach and heard voices," Papa reports. "I think it was a rebel base."

"We heard them too, meters from the house," Cristian confirms.

"We came to the beach to stay clear of the battle," Papa states. "Batista kills people who don't report these findings."

"We can't turn those men in!" Samuel pleads. "We know some of them. You know what that murderer will do to them!"

"I want you two to keep this to yourselves and pretend you don't know a thing!" Papa commands. "I'll tell the others the same. And stay away from this cause!"

Samuel takes Cristian outside to a secluded spot, "Have you told anyone that I'm helping the rebels?" he asks nervously.

"Of course not," he whispers. "But you better be careful! Batista is ordering his men to assassinate anyone who is against him."

"I know, but I have friends on the front lines, and I have to help."

"Be careful, especially at night. Spotting figures or shadows on the hills is difficult. Soldiers capture men, and you know what happens when they do!"

"I'll be careful, I promise," Samuel tries to reassure Cristian.

The next morning, six miles from Imias, on Yaterita beach, a local fisherman feels a tug on his line, as he reels in his first catch of the day. A small tuna flails for freedom as the fisherman unhooks and tosses it in a container. It's a calm morning with a clear blue sky as he casts his line.

The ripple from the sinking fishing line puts him in a trance. Suddenly, he catches movement from the corner of his eye. An object has just washed to shore. He saunters over curiously, and as he gets closer to the object, he makes an unsettling discovery. He discovers a corpse, and unable to control himself, he heaves. The pruned body has a missing eye. He looks around in desperation.

"Ayuda!" his voice cracks as he yells for help.

He leaned in closer to the body. He was trembling, but wanted to take a closer look. Realizing he knows the young rebel, he frantically runs back and forth contemplating his next move. If soldiers see him, they will interrogate him. Fear consumes him, and he flees the scene.

Later that afternoon, he confides in a friend, and word spreads to the rebel base about their dead comrade.

The next morning, the rebels frantically search the beach, but the corpse has mysteriously disappeared. The sun sits high in the late morning; hot air surrounds Samuel as he looks around to make sure no one follows. Cautious not to lose the sack dangling over his shoulder, he creeps through the vegetation to his destination.

In a small clearing, decaying trees and branches are a front to the entrance of the rebel camp. A short, stocky man, masked by dirt from his days in hiding, creeps out and flags Samuel over. They sneak into the hideout, taking a seat on a stump. Embers from a fire crackle as they warm black beans on a pot while a rebel stirs in rice.

Samuel inhales the aroma of the simmering beans, "Smells good brother."

The cook nods his head with a grin, wiping his forehead. Several other rebels rest on hammocks before their shift starts. Rifles prop alongside a pile of sticks next to a stack of homemade bombs.

"Here you go, my friend," Samuel whispers. "I snuck the food from the house." He hands the sack to his friend.

"You need to be very careful!" the rebel warns him with a mournful stare.

"What's wrong?" In many weeks of helping the rebels, Samuel had never received such a warning.

"A fisherman found your friend Carlos," the rebel explains.

A knot in the pit of Samuel's stomach gets heavier as the rebel recalls the details. He slams his fist on his thigh as he clenches his teeth. "We need to get rid of this sadistic bastard!"

"Join us up here, brother," the cook pleads. "Fidel has a plan. He's going to get that killer off our island and bring back fair elections."

Furious, he decides to do more to stop this vicious dictator. "I have to help with my family's business," Samuel informs his friend. "But I will continue to provide supplies and funds. What else do you need?"

"We need weapons," the rebel mentions.

"I'm on it," Samuel assures him.

Samuel returns home, dragging Cristian for a walk on the beach. They stop on a secluded part of the coast. Samuel shares the turn of events with his brother, his only confidant.

"I'm very worried about you!" Cristian warns.

"Remember the great times we had on this beach?" Samuel reminisces, trying to distract his big brother.

"Yes, I do!" he replies, as they recall one of their last enjoyable moments in the area.

7 - Three Rocks

Cristian and Samuel relive the last memorable time on the beach in 1955.

"Mama, we're done with our duties," Cristian informed her. "We're going to meet our friends."

"And find some girls," Samuel whispered to Cristian.

"Wait for me!" Victor, a year older than Cristian, but a couple of inches shorter, thin and not very athletic, ran after them.

"We might also borrow the jeep!" Cristian hollered as they ran out of the house with two bags of meat cloaked by their guayaberas.

Porch lights guided them down the busy línea on this typical Saturday night. Porches vibrated with bongo beats, as the strumming of guitars boomed from radios. The chattering of men and clicking of chips as they played billiards or dominos pulsed through the street. Samuel eavesdropped on their conversations.

"The crème de la crème from America gamble in the casinos of Havana. Handing all their money to those crooked gangsters and that bandit! They're making millions and what the hell do we get, CRAP!" An old man moved his domino chip as he protested.

"Cuba is turning into a drug port, while Batista profits and steals funds that should go to public health, education, and maintenance," another agreed.

"Did you hear them?" Samuel looked at Cristian.

"Just old man gossip, ignore it," Cristian reassured him.

Children ran up and down la línea. Their playful sounds echoed through the air, as Cristian took in his surroundings, embracing his tropical paradise.

Cristian, Victor, and Samuel hopped in the jeep, making their way to their destination. All the local teenagers snuck to the beach for their Saturday night gathering to eat and dance. It was the Enriquez's turn to bring the meal. Today, the entree of choice was ropa vieja and arroz, or shredded beef and rice, their specialty and a favorite of their friends. Feeling entitled to the same extravagant meals as adults; the teens looked forward to their weekend meals together.

A warm sea breeze drifted in as the brilliant moonlit sky illuminated the beach. Just past a set of palm trees that leaned out to salute the sea, the brothers stopped at the usual cooking spot. The trees provided a blockade from the sea breeze. Cristian and Victor scouted the area for sticks while Samuel arranged three rocks in the sand. Samuel arranged the cooking area, placing the sticks over the stones then started the fire. "Here you go, brother," he advised Cristian.

"Ok, I have this," Cristian informed his brothers. He let them mingle and dance while he cooked up the savory dish, as Cristian did not dance and Samuel had moves like Elvis.

"Have fun!" Samuel smirked as he patted Cristian on the back.

Cristian placed a big iron pan over the flame where he seasoned and mixed the ropa vieja as he watched couples dance. He would not dare to leave the fire for fear that a furry Cuban hutia or Cuban solenodon would smell the meat, scurry over, and devour the food.

As the evening set, Victor kept Cristian company by the crackling fire, barely heard through the laughter and music. Over 20 teens danced to the tunes blaring from the Cocaleca, a tiki hut discotheque that sat near the edge where the beach meets the river.

As the night ended, the brothers strolled the beach and headed towards a set of boulders. The waves crashed against the rocks, blocking out the noise from the Cocaleca, as the brothers splashed around in the foaming tide. On the soft sand, they joked and laughed as they reminisced on their last summer together. The Three Amigos parted ways for a while as Cristian and Victor headed off to the University. Back on the beach, a seagull dives down by their feet, snapping Cristian and Samuel out of their flashback.

8 – Santiago

Cuba is a tropical paradise for celebrities like Frank Sinatra, who entertain the Batista regime and the wealthy. Abundant with luxurious hotels, nightclubs, restaurants, and casinos, Hollywood and Americans are fascinated by Cuba's glamor, tropical climate, and spectacular music. Elites like Ava Gardner and Frank Sinatra fly down for the weekend to amuse themselves in the wild nightlife. Everyone but the Cuban citizens are having a great time. Glamorous hotels rise with government money meant for the poor or sick. Cubans want to benefit from these industries, and students want to experience the exciting life, but the fight for their country takes precedence. Tourists are oblivious to the police bloodshed that keeps protesters under control.

1957

On the beach, the brothers continue their conversation, "I missed you guys after you went to the University," Samuel informs Cristian after recalling their last memorable summer on their beach. *He remembers how lost he was without Cristian*, but keeps that memory to himself.

The brothers march back to the beach shack to continue their work, hoping no one realizes how long they were gone.

"We're going to work in the fincas," Cristian informs Mama. The brothers flee avoiding contact and questions from others.

Later that evening, Cristian and Samuel finish the work in the coffee finca. With the work completed, the brothers lead the mules down the hills to graze. Cristian and Samuel cherish the mule rides, always volunteering for the peaceful walks and trips to the pastures.

A golden horizon lights their trail as the sun starts to set this evening. Plumes of clouds in the distance announce a clear night ahead. The scent of the lush grass surrounds them, along with new sounds of nature sprouting as the Cuban Treefrog awakens. Horses and cows browse in the area, casually glancing up to check the guests in their surroundings. The abundance of vegetation provides privacy for the brothers' deep conversations, as they reflect on their lives and plan their future. They take their time on the walk back to absorb their serene surroundings.

That evening, back at the beach shelter, the constellations light up the sky as night sets. A distinct whistle in the distance grabs Cristian's attention. Stepping out the back door, he sees a silhouette running towards the river. With a sack on his back, the man dodges trees and looks back checking for guards. *A neighbor in town must have given the rebels food,* Cristian thinks to himself, as he observes the rebel cutting through the river to reach the mountains.

"The rebels have made camp in the mountains," Papa says joining Cristian outside.

"In the evenings, I've noticed they make their way into town to get supplies and food," Cristian informs him.

"I know a few friends in town sneak to the mountains and give them necessities. The rebels will not rest until they take all the guard headquarters," Samuel briefs Papa and Cristian. "Batista's army has tried to penetrate the rebel's bases in the mountains but hasn't been successful."

"How do you know so much?" Papa asks Samuel.

"Friends told me," he says hoping Papa wouldn't ask more questions.

"I want you boys to stay away from any political or war causes! Do you hear me?" Papa warns them. "After the corrupt elections Batista held, anyone who opposes him is tortured or assassinated."

"People don't want him to get away with it. He can't use fraud and intimidation to win an election!" Samuel fumes.

"I understand, but we are staying out of it!" Papa commands. "Batista is after all rebels, and for some reason, this idiot and lunatic also considers being a student a severe crime." With five students in the household, Papa panics. "Stay out of this war!"

"Okay, Papa," Samuel responds.

"We'll stay out of it," Cristian assures him.

They do not like lying to Papa, but they do not intend to keep their word. It's not in them to sit idly by as a dictator destroys their paradise home and takes away their freedom. Samuel has many friends involved in this fight, and he feels strongly about the cause. Cristian feels compelled to keep an eye on his little brother. They plan to help the rebels, being very cautious to keep the family out of harm's way.

Samuel continues to sneak food and supplies into the mountains, with Cristian covering for him while keeping a close eye on his little brother.

One morning, a friend of Papa stops by the Honradez. He does not come in to shop.

"I've heard some news about Samuel," he informs Papa.

"What do you mean?" he inquires.

"The government is aware of his allegiance with the rebels," he cautions Papa. "They might pick him up for treason, or worse!"

"Thank you, my friend; I'll take care of him." After the man leaves, Papa slams his hand on the counter. He begins to pace as fear takes over him when he imagines his son's fate if caught.

Papa runs to their shelter at the beach to tell Mama of the information he just received. For Samuel's safety, Papa will take him to a house they own in Santiago de Cuba. Despite her worries, Mama agrees to go and leave the rest of the family.

"Batista's guards heard of your involvement with the rebels, and they're looking for you," Papa tells Samuel about his friend's warning. "We're going to Santiago!"

Sweat drips down Cristian's forehead as he places a suitcase in the jeep. Samuel squeezes by him, stacking a bag on top. Their vehicle races down the beach kicking up sand. They cut through to a gravel road, heading to the dock. An employee waits on the boat to take them to Santiago. Papa has brought Cristian to help Mama keep an eye on Samuel. The four waste no time getting on the boat and shipping out.

Santiago, a town on the southern coast, west of Imias, houses one of the family's biggest branch stores. As months go by in Santiago, the young men get very comfortable, being near many of their professors and friends from the university. Samuel's involvement got them here. Cautious not to get caught again, the brothers tend to all their duties at home and the store before meeting with friends.

"We're going to the café," Samuel informs Mama, hoping to keep his parents from getting suspicious.

"Be careful," she responds. "Don't get back too late."

The café bustles in Santiago, a much bigger town with more traffic than Imias. Cubans involved in the cause are camouflaged as they mingle. Cristian and Samuel spot their friends, and the brothers split up.

Many rebels have gone underground, and funds are necessary to get resources for them to stay in hiding. The charismatic Samuel has a way with words and collaborates with two other university students to collect funds.

Cristian works with a group to help rebels being hunted by Batista, leave the island. The group meets with local businesspeople to arrange hideouts and transportation.

9 – Town Square

The Cuban national debt rises. Cubans have had enough of the Dictator, and the revolution flares throughout the island. Images sent to the world of the grand hotels and casinos, luxury homes and cars, and celebrity parties are an illusion. Cubans lack medical help. In the country towns, children are exploited for work, as they do the dangerous task of cutting down sugar cane, to keep the family from dying of hunger. Many live in dilapidated wooden bunkhouses with thatch roofs and no electricity. People all over Cuba get involved in an island-wide work stoppage. They bomb bathroom stalls and garbage cans to scare away tourists and impact tourism. Money from the casinos and travel industry showers on Batista and the Mafia. Many people find great hope in Fidel. They want a change, and right now, anyone will do.

With Mama and the brothers safe in Santiago, Papa returns to Imias to check on the rest of the family. Battle blasts have dwindled in the evenings. With less commotion in town, hope for normalcy fills the air.

Sea waves splash and sand flings around as a half-built sandcastle sits on the edge of the beach. The Enriquez grandchildren playfully splash in the sea when Alejandro, Cristian's older brother, calls them in for lunch.

There is a loud knock at the door.

"We have a message from the government," a general at the door shouts.

"What is it?" Alejandro, a tall, tanned, muscular man, responds.

"Everyone needs to evacuate Imias!" a stocky general in his military gear commands.

"Why?"

"They're going to be more attacks on the barracks."

Alejandro worries for the family and sends his oldest daughter to the store to give Papa the news.

"A general came by and told us we have to leave the area because of more attacks!" she cries to Papa.

"What, not again!" he cries in disbelief.

"Papi wanted me to tell you that we're starting to pack."

"Ok, we'll close things up here and head home."

With their hopes shattered, the men move quickly. Everyone helps seal up the store, with Papa torn between leaving his home and business, but will not risk his family's safety.

On the beach, the family scurries to pack. Clothes, toys, food, and other valuable items bulge out of the jeep, truck, and minibus. Mama will be surprised to see the caravan pull up in Santiago.

Once they arrive in Santiago, Papa preoccupies himself with the other businesses on the island to distract himself from the properties in Imias. *What will they find when they return?* He wonders in torment.

Back in Imias, rebels camp in the mountains, waiting for night to fall. They find shelter in a small clearing of the woods. Military hats shade their scalps from the Caribbean sun. In their camouflage clothing and dirt-stained, half unbuttoned shirts, they nourish themselves with a warm meal prepared over a campfire. They take turns heating rice and beans, while a chicken roasts on a stick.

Rebels creep into town when night arrives. They make their attack on the police station, barricading themselves behind sandbags, buildings, and trees. Gunshots echo through the city as men wail in pain. Injured rebels are carried back to camp while others sneak into stores and businesses in town looking for supplies. The rebel's general, a professor from the university and a close friend of Samuel, leads the men into town.

"Don't touch the Honradez!" the general points to the Enriquez store. "Only take what we need from the others."

Meanwhile in Santiago, away from the turmoil in Imias, a sense of peace finally sets in for the family. The bustling city provides an additional diversion for the family.

Samuel wakes up, quickly getting ready to start his day. He walks out onto the wooden porch, admiring the view to the east. The majestic mountains sit peacefully, cloaking the unrest living on them. As he heads west down the quiet hill, a stray cat keeps him company on his walk to the town square, the Parque Cespedes. Generously sized brick and stucco homes fill the street. Bright Caribbean colors adorn the exterior elevations of the houses set flush next to one another. Entryways greet visitors in various forms, from wooden porches to Spanish style entrances.

As Samuel approaches the town square, pedestrian and automobile traffic start to pick up. He reaches the main road and crosses the busy street to the square. The town square in Santiago brims with people on their way to work or gathering for social events.

Samuel reaches the top of the stairs, scouting the park. Children flutter through, and couples affectionately stroll. He makes his way to the other side waiting in front of the Carlos Manuel de Céspedes Monument to find a rebel friend. Samuel will get directions on purchasing fire arms.

"We've taken the barracks and captured the survivors!" his rebel friend celebrates.

"Hal-le-lu-yah!" Samuel revels.

"We have more than 80 captives. Batista has less men to wreak havoc on our island."

"Thank you, my friend! My family will be glad to hear we can go back home."

Samuel returns home to tell Papa the good news. That night, at dinner, Papa informs the rest of the family that it appears to be safe to move back to Imias. They start to make plans for their return.

The boys decide to go back to Imias, as well, since they cannot continue their studies yet. Samuel knows many people in Imias who are rebels and more involved in the revolution than those in Santiago. He will stay involved until peace is restored all over the island, and they can return to school.

10 – The Horse

*Unemployment rates rise, especially among college
graduates. Students begin to riot, as they are fed up with
racial and gender discrimination, universities being
shutting down, and repression of freedom of press and
public meetings. Batista controls the biggest military
machine in the history of Cuba. The Bureau of
Investigation, Secret Police, and others are ordered to kill
any who oppose. Students secretly pass out propaganda,
placing it on top of buildings for it to fly away. Outside
universities, students march with banners, running when
the police begin to beat them with weapons or to shoot.
Bystanders yell, "Murderers, henchmen!"*

Back in Imias, Cristian and Samuel rise early. They
share the spacious room containing two sets of bunk beds,
with Victor and, at times, Alejandro and his family. After
getting out of bed, Cristian dresses, sliding on his shoes.
On his way out, he picks up the urinal pan to empty in the
outhouse. Walking out, he sees Papa sitting at the dining
room table, reading a paper. He tip-toes down the hall to
avoid waking up those in the other bedrooms. His oldest
brother, Alberto, and his wife and children stay with the

family from time to time, taking a break from tending one of the other stores on the island.

Cristian makes his way across the kitchen's concrete floor, stepping outside to the backyard. It's a humid morning as he treads across the patchy lawn to the outhouse. He leaves the urinal pan out for cleaning and disinfecting.

The spacious backyard stirs with chickens, pigs, and sheep. Friends from a neighboring town kept an eye on the property when it was vacant. At the northeast corner, a Kapok tree guards the chicken feed. Cristian ventures behind the majestic sacred tree to uncover the corn bucket, reaching in and scooping a can full of grain. As he sprinkles it on the ground for the chickens, he hears Samuel beginning his chores.

Back towards the house, Samuel fills a bucket of water out of the spigot. He carefully hauls the bucket into the house, putting it on the rustic kitchen counter next to the sink.

"Here you go, Mama," Samuel says.

"Thank you, mijo," Mama responds.

She will use the water for cooking and washing dishes. The only room in the house with a faucet is the bathroom, which only houses a soaking tub. Cristian steps into the kitchen, spotting Mama with her long braided hair preparing breakfast on the homemade wooden island. She turns off the burner to the brewed café as he kisses her on the cheek and pours himself a cup. Cautious not to spill, he sits next to Samuel at the table with a piece of toast. He savors his café as it wakes him up. Meanwhile Mama meticulously prepares her workspace with potatoes, carrots and malanga, a vegetable from the potato family. Swiftly, the brothers drop their dishes in the sink and head through the house to unlock the store.

"See you in the afternoon," they dismiss themselves with a kiss on Mama's cheek.

"Adios," the tough countrywoman responds.

In the store, Cristian opens the front door, stepping onto the wooden porch as he spots a neighbor across the street setting up the café. He gazes down the sloping road past the adjoining homes and businesses, painted in bright baby blue and pale pink colors. Palm trees sprout out behind the buildings at the edge of the road. The view comes to a halt at the glorious mountains. Overcast skies and low flying birds warn of the storm that will arrive later in the day.

Cristian stands on la línea, inhaling the soothing sea breeze. Now back home, a sense of relief overwhelms him as the town starts to come back to life. Locals move back, and sandbags disappear.

Samuel begins to work at the produce display. He removes the potato sacks on the storage boxes to expose fresh lemons, limes, and potatoes. Cristian heads to the back of the building, snatching the rolling cart. Cautiously to prevent bruising, he pulls boxes of produce from the refrigerator, placing them on the wagon. Leading the cart to the front of the building, he starts organizing the items on the display boxes, then snatches the watering can to give the lettuce and carrots a light shower.

The battle continues on the island, but life must go on. Later in the day, Papa, Cristian, Samuel, and a couple of employees head out on the pick-up truck. A shipment of supplies has arrived on the boat to replenish the store. Papa takes a seat between the driver and passenger. Cristian and an employee jump in the bed of the truck, while Samuel clowns around, and then decides to stand on the running board of the passenger side.

"I forgot something," Samuel yells, running inside.

"Hurry up," Papa commands. "We have a lot of work to do."

Upon returning, Samuel jumps on the running board of the driver side this time. They get on their way, and

Samuel teases Papa on his choice of music. He ignores his son and continues to tune the radio.

As they drive down la línea, suddenly they hear a plane flying above. Samuel looks up to see the aircraft flying away. The group continues on the quiet road leading to the beach as the plane flies overhead. A few minutes pass when they hear the sound of a low flying aircraft again. The engine gets louder, causing Cristian to look up noticing the aircraft descending slowly towards them.

"What the hell's going on?" Papa roars. The men look out the window and up to the sky.

"It's a government plane," Cristian points up.

A shower of bullets falls on the truck as it comes under attack by the plane. The driver swerves, running off the road. Everyone but the front passenger jump out in utter confusion.

"Run for cover!" Papa orders.

Cristian looks around assessing the situation as he counts heads. The man on the passenger side wails in pain. Cristian runs to check on him.

"Samuel, help me!" Cristian pleads.

"What's wrong?" Papa asks.

"He's shot," Cristian yells.

"I'm coming!" Papa announces.

"No! Find cover." Samuel tells Papa as he runs over to help Cristian.

They carry the injured employee off the truck, following the others into the field. The group runs behind a nearby tree, sitting quietly and waiting. The plane swings back around looking for them, but does not spot them and flies away. They lie there, evaluating the situation.

Cristian's heart beats a million beats per second. Why are we being attacked, he ponders. He scouts the area. Two men lie on the ground praying Hail Mary, while Papa watches the sky waiting for another ambush. Samuel kneels next to the injured man as he applies pressure on the wound in his right thigh. Cristian crawls over to console the crying man, noticing a petrified look in Samuel's eyes.

"You okay!" Cristian pats Samuel on the back.

"This could have been me. Probably worse, if I did not move to the other side of the truck," Samuel whispers.

"You have an angel watching over you."

"Do I? Why do I feel guilty? It should have been me! He has kids. What if this injury is life-threatening?"

"He's going to be fine, you'll see."

"Anyone see or hear anything?" Papa calls out.

"No," Cristian responds.

"Do you think the town is under attack?" Papa worries that the family is in danger.

"Remember what happened to those university students?" Cristian murmurs to Samuel.

"Yeah," Samuel acknowledges out of breath.

"What if that happens to us?" Cristian asks.

11 - Newspaper

Frank Paiz, a well-known activist, is ambushed and assassinated. Cubans swarm the streets of Santiago in protest. The rebel, Fidel, claims he will seek social justice, democratic government, free press, and free elections. Fidel has rebels plant bombs in nightclubs and theaters to sabotage Batista's government. Civilians are injured and killed in the blasts, which Fidel claims is collateral damage.

Hiding behind the tree with the other men, Cristian and Samuel recall the events of March 13, 1957. They remember that on a calm afternoon, groups of university students from Directorio Revolucionario Estudiantil (DRE) and Federación Estudiantíl Universitaria (FEU) secretly assembled. One group made its way to the Presidential Palace to overthrow Batista. Simultaneously, the other group headed to the CMQ radio station to go on air to announce the fall of Batista.

Outside the Palace, the first group encountered an unexpected barricade of guards. They panicked, contemplating the tragedy that would follow. The second group would announce Batista's fall, but he would be safe.

As they waited, brainstorming a new plan of attack, the guards suddenly disappeared. They made their move to attack the Palace. Upon entering, they discovered that Batista got away.

Terror flowed through the rebels' veins. The entire group was in danger, as Batista showed no mercy to anyone that opposed him. Everyone went into hiding. The head of the group rushed to the university to seek refuge. He reached the grand stairs leading to the campus, and with urgency, he began his climb when a swarm of bullets pierced his body. The police left his corpse lying on a flight of stairs as a warning to others. Seven others from the group found refuge in an apartment on Humbold 7 St near the Malecon, Oceanfront Boulevard.

Days passed, and they continued to hide in fear. Fellow rebels and friends secretly provided them with food and necessities.

A few weeks later, in the apartment, several of the men huddled, discussing their next move. Another sat at the table reading the newspaper. A noise startled the man, forcing him to look up to the stampede of guards storming in. Bullets pierced flesh, furniture, and walls as one by one the young men's bodies fell to the ground. Lifeless bodies lay in a pool of blood.

"How is he?" Papa crawls over to his sons, interrupting the brothers' recollection on the slaughter of the university students.

"The bleeding seems to be under control, but he looks pale," Samuel informs Papa while adding pressure to the man's wound.

Samuel focuses back on Cristian, "That will not happen to us!" Samuel assures him.

Papa quietly hashes out a plan with all the men as they continue to hide behind the tree.

Suddenly, Samuel spots a man on a horse trotting, unaware of the raid that just took place in this field.

"Help!" the men yell, waving their arms.

He stops, and they quickly explain what happened. The farmer allows Samuel to borrow the horse and he gallops back to town for help. The local doctor tells Samuel to get the injured man to the hospital.

The nearest hospital is in the town of Baracoa, miles away. Samuel races back with a car, and, along with Papa, they take the injured man to the hospital. Cristian and the other men, once again, attempt the trip to the beach while constantly looking up at the sky. They arrive safely at the port and load the supplies on the truck. The men and goods arrive at the store in one piece. When Papa returns from

the hospital, he gauges the damage. The attack leaves
bullet holes in the truck, Papa with some shrapnel
punctures, and an employee with a minor injury.

12 – Navidad

The revolution started with a few men then grew to almost 40,000. Batista fueled the revolution by terrorizing Cubans. His corrupt regime had stolen $500 million from the country. The government had executed thousands of civic leaders and young adults. Government guards are ordered to bury people alive and perform torturous acts. These included taking out people's eyes, sticking nails in their heads, pulling off their nails, and limbs. People are forced to be silent by even having their lips sewn shut.

Winter arrives cooling the scorched island as Navidades, or Christmas, draws near. The Enriquez's warehouse in town overflows. Dolls and toy cars sit on shelves waiting for their next home. Stacks of Christmas lights and garland are in short supply as locals stock up for the Holiday season, with all the extra holiday supplies, the warehouse transforms into a temporary store.

On Noche Buena, Christmas Eve, the family gets to work early in the morning. Alejandro's children stir out of bed when they hear a commotion. A stampede of footsteps and squealing cause them to peek out of their bedroom. A pig dashes by, with Papa and the boys on its tail. They chase the swine for several minutes, throwing chairs around as it sneaks under the dining table. Finally, the animal is out-smarted when Samuel tackles it.

Papa has the older boys help him slaughter and clean what was their biggest pig. They transport it to a homemade caja china, a roasting box. An employee feeds a steel pipe through the pig, propping the pipe on each side by two steel posts, which sit in a charcoal-filled pit.

With the morning house chores complete, Cristian heads to work. It's usually his job to handle sales at the warehouse during Navidades, but Papa has special assignments today. For his first task, Cristian loads the truck at the warehouse with bananas to be transported to the store.

Next, he heads down to the beach to pick up merchandise from the boat. As Cristian drives off, the distinct, joyful sounds of the town getting ready for the festivities exhilarate him. Pedestrians walk cautiously with arms overloaded, while locals chat and prepare for the evening's events.

The drive down to the beach always feels therapeutic with palm trees swaying in the calm sea breeze, the soothing call of el Toti as it soars in the air from its tree, and the Caribbean sun generating a mild temperature. He arrives at the dock, where the boat patiently waits. Cristian heads up the ramp to unload it, while an employee helps to pack all the supplies on the truck.

"How was the trip?" Cristian asks the worker, picking up a box.

"The sea is quiet," the man replies. "I'm glad it was quick and easy. I couldn't wait to get back."

"Yeah, let's hurry up. I'm anxious to get home."

The two take the inventory to the warehouse, where Papa and Samuel help store the items. Papa looks around to an almost barren building. A few lights sit lonely on a shelf with other limited Christmas supplies, the sign of a successful season as the men close up. There is a quiet excitement as the crew walks back to the house to join everyone in the backyard.

Cristian beams as he scans the full yard where the lechón asado, the pig has been roasting for hours. Employees tended to it during the day, slowly spinning it over the fire pit. His mouth waters hearing the crackle and sizzle, as the skin starts to crisp.

"I have this," Cristian tells the man cooking the pig. "Go get a drink and take a break."

"Thank you," the worker responds.

"And get me a drink while you're at it," Cristian jokes.

Wisps of smoke glide through the backyard, as they carry the aroma of garlic and cumin from the roasting pig. Laughter fills the air, as the men enjoy cold beverages.

The women cheerfully tend to the dishes inside. Mama creates her famed mojo, gravy, an old Cuban recipe of naranja agria, bitter orange juice and garlic. Cristian's sisters help with the savory meal as they smash plantains for tostones and fry them twice. The house fills with the intoxicating aroma coming from the old cooktop. Someone watches over the congris, rice and black beans, while others work on the yuca, a potato like vegetable until the flame goes out on the stove.

Mama summons the boys over to help her. Cristian and Samuel hustle back to the backyard, retrieving a tall white tank of gas. With caution, they haul it into the kitchen, replacing the empty container that powers the oven and stove.

Radiant lights adorn the streets and their house, as lively romantic rumba and salsa music fills the air, brightening everyone's spirits.

The family and employees sit down together for this grand yearly banquet. The dinner table vibrates with merry conversations and giggles. Papa sips his favorite, El Gaitero de Villaricioso Cider, an alcoholic beverage that has been around for centuries. The older boys enjoy Benedictine and Chartreuse Amarillo, traditional liqueurs of Spain.

After everyone devours the Cena de Navidad, this Christmas Eve dinner, Mama brings out applesauce and turrones, nougats from Spain. They enjoy each other's company without any worries until the late hours of the evening.

13 – Rio

*The United States withdraws support for Batista
and refuses to let him seek refuge in America. At midnight
on December 31, 1958, Batista flees the island with his
cabinet and millions of Cuban dollars. Fidel Castro and
the rebels have defeated him. Cubans finally have a sense
of hope.*

*In an interview, Fidel announces, "I do not want
power. My role in the revolution is over. Now I will do
what is best for the country. If stepping down is best, then I
will step down." Before he steps down, he states he has
more work to do.*

1958

It is Noche de Año Nuevo, New Year's Eve.
Cristian finishes his breakfast, then begins the routine
quarterly maintenance on the family's vehicles. After
dragging his blue dented toolbox from underneath his bed,
he walks into the store. From the auto supply shelves, he
places oil filters and Castrol oil in his work crate.

He heads outside to a street filled with pedestrians.
Men spend the day working in local businesses, while

women tend to their homes. Out in front of the Honradez, the truck's radio blares the rhythmic mambo music Cristian enjoys. Underneath the vehicle, he unscrews the filter as the oil drips into the pan. With care, he twists the brand new oil filter into place. He slides across on the creeper. As he crawls out from underneath the vehicle, the winter air energizes him. He pours the new oil with precision. After finishing his first vehicle, he moves on to the next. In the early afternoon, he packs up his tools and cleans up, while Samuel finishes his chores in the store.

"Let's go, Cristian," hollers Samuel. "Hurry up!"

"Stop yelling and help me clean up!" Cristian barks.

After the boys wrap up their duties, they head to the kitchen for a quick bite. Mama has a stack of Cuban sandwiches, slices of ham and strips of marinated pork spilling out the sides, ready for everyone.

Samuel kisses Mama on the cheek, "Gracias!" yanking a sandwich from the plate.

Cristian kisses her on the forehead. "Gracias!" gulping his sandwich.

"Slow down, mijo," Mama says.

Scarfing down his food, Cristian reports, "I'm starving, and we have to go. Our friends are waiting."

Cristian and Samuel grab a Malta, Spanish pop, for the road as they head on their adventure down by the river, Rio de Imias.

The Rio de Imias flows parallel to la línea, on the north side, then makes a sharp turn south to join the Caribbean Sea. North of the river on luscious hills, the Enriquez family nurtures fruit orchards. La línea ends in Imias where it meets another gravel road that heads south to greet the white sandy beach.

This afternoon, a waterfall welcomes the boys as they arrive at the river. A green backsplash of mangrove trees guards it on the north side, sprinkling it with a rainbow of tropical foliage. A few friends have gathered, waiting patiently for the brothers.

"Let the party begin," Samuel announces as they arrive at the river.

"The guest of honor has arrived," Cristian says, resting his arm on Samuel.

Samuel shoves Cristian off, and a friend tackles Samuel. The young men jump and splash, running across rocks that washed downstream. The two brothers are inseparable, with Cristian always keeping an eye on his baby brother, but right now Samuel is nowhere to be found.

"Samuel!" everyone calls out.

"Where the hell are you?" Cristian calls.

Mangrove roots camouflage Samuel as Cristian walks past. Samuel catches him by surprise.

"You jerk!" Cristian yells.

They splash around in the water as the rest of the boys dive on the jokester, all laughing.

The sun lowers in the horizon, a sign for all to return home. Before they head back, they bathe in the river; then Cristian and Samuel retrace their steps down the silent rio. They arrive at the mouth of the river before it pours into the sapphire Caribbean Sea. Cristian pauses along the edge of the beach, hypnotized by the clear water that meets a bright blue horizon. To the east, a few cloud plumes breeze by in front of a descending sun.

"Let's go," Samuel orders Cristian. "I bet I can beat you this time!"

"You haven't before. What makes you think you can do it today?" Cristian teases. Cristian selects a smooth rock. With a twist to the wrist, he tosses the stone in the sea. One, two, three, four, five skips. "Beat that!"

Samuel chooses his rock, takes a couple of test swings, and then releases the stone. One, two, three, the stone sinks.

Cristian's loud, contagious laugh mocks Samuel.

"Just wait, I'll kick your ass one of these days," Samuel insists.

They continue their rock-skipping competition on the radiant and serene sea as they walk along the beach with its lush sea grape trees growing on the sandy shore. Large leaves house the exotic green and purple grapes that flourish in the sandy soil. The brothers take a break from rock skipping to pick sea grapes for a snack before heading home.

In town, customers spill into Honradez purchasing last minute ingredients for their dishes. Locals prepare for the annual Enriquez New Year's Eve party. Women slip on their party dresses, and men put on their formal guayabera.

Back at home, Cristian dresses up for the party.

"I'm going to catch up with some friends before the party," Cristian informs Samuel. "Cover for me."

"Fine," Samuel waves as he brushes his hair. "You owe me."

"Yeah, Yeah." Cristian ducks out to have a drink at the bar with a friend. When walking in, the bright rainbow lights of the jukebox call to him. His fingers dance, jumping from one button to another in search of the right song from the wide selection. After making his choice, he goes to hang out with a group of friends at the counter.

Cristian pats his friend on the back. "Ah, there he is," his friend joyfully announces.

"Sorry, got tied up at home," Cristian reports.

"Can I have another beer?" his friend requests, waving the bartender over.

"I'll be right back," Cristian says abruptly. He starts chatting as he discreetly snuggles up to Sara, his crush. The couple joins the rest of the group as they continue talking and drinking until Cristian realizes the time; the party at home has begun. Everyone will wonder where he is.

Frantically, he rushes home, hopeful no one noticed his absence. As he reaches the door, he begins to feel dizzy. He stumbles, creeping over to the side of the house. Unable to control it, he vomits in the bushes, hoping all the alcohol is out of his system and that no one sees him. Papa would be furious to see him in this state.

He staggers to the backyard, splashes water from the spigot on his face, and rinses his mouth. Making his way in the house, he notices the pot of café Mama always has ready on the stove. *Perhaps a cup will wake him up*, he thinks to himself. After sipping the café, he forces himself to mingle, joining in the laughter and joyous festivities.

The house packs with family, friends, and neighbors, as Cristian joins conversations, and he makes his way through the house. Despite not feeling well, he forces himself to stay up until midnight. He doesn't want to miss one of his favorite times of the year.

Several minutes before the clock strikes twelve, Mama and Papa hand each guest twelve grapes, a Cuban tradition handed down from Spain. Everyone has a grape to bring prosperity and health for each month of the coming year.

"Feliz Año Nuevo!" everyone shouts.

Noisemaker toots blast through the air. Cheers fill the room as loved ones hug and kiss. The family says goodbye to 1958 and pray for a peaceful 1959.

14 – Social Butterfly

With an entourage and caravan of tanks and military vehicles, Fidel tours the island celebrating his victory. A rifle hangs over his shoulder as Fidel stands in a jeep waving, with a cigar in his mouth. Crowds cheer in the streets as he parades himself from one city to another. At the University of Havana, Fidel holds an assembly, declaring "Armas, Para Que." Questioning the citizens why they need weapons. Cubans believe they no longer need guns and turn them in. He promises freedom of speech, free press and free elections in less than a year. The people feel a sense of relief as the dictatorship has fallen.

1959

Holiday festivities end as the island begins celebrating a new era in 1959. Cristian starts work at his standard time, but traffic is slow in the store today, so Alejandro takes over for him as he heads to the warehouse. He unloads the truck that came in from San Antonio, taking out automotive parts and cleaning supplies. An employee helps him place all the items on their proper shelf. Cristian checks the other shelves for items low in stock and fills out the inventory list.

As quitting time nears on Friday night, everyone cleans the warehouse to close up the store. Papa left the two oldest Enriquez boys in charge for a couple of days while he went to inspect the store in Veguita. Several times a year he goes to examine his other facilities throughout the island. Anytime he heads out on business, Alejandro and Alberto, the two older brothers, are watchdogs and take care of the family, house, and business.

Cristian, Victor, and Samuel begin their trek to the bar, to celebrate their return to Havana. While walking down the street monkeying around, they spot a friend who joins them. Parading down the road, they spot girls sitting and gossiping on the stairs of their front porches.

"Hello, señoritas." Samuel whistles and salutes the young ladies.

"Hi, Samuel," a short, blonde classmate flirts back. "Come over. We're having café."

"Sorry ladies, we are meeting our brothers."

"Bring them too. We'll put on some music," the brunette friend announces. Samuel's handsome features, vibrant eyes, and gallant personality always charm the ladies. He puts them in a trance with the irresistible gleam in his eyes.

The men continue on their walk, coming up to the house of Ana, on whom Victor has a crush. They decide to stop to see if she wants to join them at the bar. Ana dashes inside as soon as she sees them coming.

Samuel knocks on the door. "Can we talk to Ana?" he asks her little sister.

"She's sleeping," she arrogantly responds.

"I just saw her out here," he retorts.

"Goodbye!" She slams the door.

Fuming, Samuel knocks again. Cristian pats him on the shoulder, pointing to a disheartened Victor. "You know how strict her dad is," Samuel consoles his disappointed brother as they keep walking.

The men arrive at their favorite bar in town, a rustic, small building next to the owner's house, where a jukebox in the front greets them. In the small kitchen at the back of the building, the chef carves the pig roast. Several tables and chairs fill the cozy bar. At one of the tables, they spot their two older brothers.

As they walk over, Samuel spots a couple of friends by the bar.

"I'll be with you guys in a minute," he tells his brothers. "I'm going to say hi to my friends."

"Hurry up!" Alejandro says.

"Papa is right," Alejandro tells his brothers. "That social butterfly will probably become a politician, always entertaining everyone he runs into."

"Come with me to the bar," Alejandro pats Cristian on the back.

"Give me two sodas," Cristian asks the bartender.

"Give me five beers," Alejandro interrupts.

"Ok, my friend," the bartender responds, quickly grabbing five bottles. He pops off the tops and puts them on the counter.

Alejandro hands one to Cristian, while grinning he says, "Here, I know you like them."

The brothers drink and toast to a new era with the democratic government Cubans have been fighting and waiting for. They enjoy their last evening together before Cristian and Samuel return to their studies.

"So, when you two are done with your studies and are making the big bucks," Alejandro teases, "make sure you come back home to share that wealth."

"I'm going to drive back in my brand new convertible," Cristian states.

"I'll be in the passenger side throwing hundred dollar bills at everyone in tow," Samuel laughs.

The group doesn't realize this will be the last time they are all together.

15 – The Keys

Most Mob bosses panic, fleeing the island after their security guard disappears. Some decide to stay, trying to befriend Fidel. They hope to work out a deal with him, as they had with the previous government, but he wants nothing to do with the Mafia. Fidel orders his rebels to shut down all casinos, incarcerate mobsters, and any people that were part of Batista's regime. Large crowds of Cubans fill a stadium. Witnesses take turns in front of judges and cameras, pointing fingers and yelling out the men's crimes. One by one, the bandits are sentenced to assassination. Escorted to the fields, the convicted men stand in front of pre-dug gravesites. They stand hoping for a savior as a priest gives them their last rites. The firing squad holds their rifles at eye level. Shots fire as corpses bend in half, falling into the pit. Word quickly spreads through the island of Fidel's illegal and cruel actions. Concern rises again in Cubans.

1959

The brothers head back to Havana. Now that the revolution is over, Cristian and Samuel are anxious to return to school.

"Adios, mijos," Mama weeps as she kisses and hugs her boys. "Be good, call, and write home often."

"We will Mama," Cristian reassures her.

"Let's go, boys," Papa announces. "The bus won't wait."

"We're coming," Samuel responds, kissing Mama on the cheek.

Papa and the brothers drive to the bus station. "I'll send you money weekly for expenses," Papa informs the brothers.

"Thanks, Papa!" Cristian replies.

"Let me know if you need more for school or books."

"Okay," Samuel answers.

Pulling up to the station, Papa stresses, "Stay in contact. You know how Mama worries." Papa pats his sons on their shoulders, a subtle way for him to show his pride in his boys.

"We will," Cristian reassures.

The brothers jump out of the jeep, grabbing their suitcases. Waving to Papa, they climb into the bus. Samuel leads them down the aisle. Cristian nods at a mother burping her crying baby. He smiles at a couple snuggling and it reminds him of the last time he saw Sara, at the local bar with his brothers. He will miss her, but can't wait to return to Havana. Samuel finds an empty seat and he waves at Papa as they sit down.

"Finally, we can get our degrees," Cristian smiles at Samuel.

"And start making some money to spend in the nightclubs and casinos," Samuel adds.

"*Aaahhh* the nightclubs. I know how much you love to dance," Cristian gives Samuel a shove. "Pablo will be waiting for us. He's got a great restaurant he wants us to try."

They make plans for their bright new future on their trip to Havana. At the bus depot, Cristian spots Pablo waving. They cross the street and drop their suitcases to embrace their friend. The men make their way down a crowded street, past a man puffing on his cigar as he leans on the stucco wall. A group of pedestrians gathers at a corner immersed in laughter and conversation. Parents hold their children's hands as they wait for the traffic signal to change. On the wrought iron balconies above, a couple of ladies wave to their dates on the street. The brothers and their friend make their way to the restaurant to celebrate their arrival. The congestion energizes Cristian and Samuel and they feel right at home.

The next morning, Cristian looks up the tall flight of concrete steps, smiling, imagining himself in a lecture hall. An unusually quiet campus captures their curiosity as they climb the steps.

At the records office, Cristian greets the receptionist and asks for their college program certificates.

"What do you mean you don't have them?" Cristian asks in a panicked tone.

"All the education certificates are lost," the woman mumbles.

Samuel fumes, "How could this happen?" He slams his fist on the counter. "What is the University going to do about this?"

Batista left behind one last insult to injury.

The brothers stay in Havana and register for new courses, in hopes the new government irons all this out. A local guesthouse becomes their new home. Cristian finds work at a ceramics factory and Samuel at the post office.

Meanwhile, Fidel begins drastic changes on the island. He nationalizes the American businesses of electricity, telephone, sugarcane, and all other private companies. They are all now the property of the Cuban government and his actions stir up tension with the United States. Fidel sends his government henchmen to confiscate properties with his family's finca as the first victim. Disturbed and upset, that her property no longer belongs to her; with somber eyes, Fidel's mom drives past her finca in her jeep with her belongings.

After several months pass, Papa makes his monthly trip to the store in San Ignacio. Rumors spread through the island of the Agrarian Reform Act, the nationalizing of Cuban companies. Papa rushes to Imias to guard his empire in case the gossip is true.

Several days later, back home in Imias, Papa is helping an employee stock shelves, when he notices an unfamiliar jeep pulling up. Two men in green military suits emerge from the dark olive vehicle. A third creeps out, flicking his cigar on the ground. Papa suspects they are G2s, government officials. They march in, surveying the store. Their boots sound like drums hitting the gravel, and Papa feels like his heart is about to jump out of his chest. *Why are they here*, he worries that his worst fears will come true?

"Who is the owner of this property?" a tall, intimidating man with a mustache demands.

"I am," Papa responds.

"Your property is being nationalized," he says as he hands Papa a document. "You are to leave this property immediately!"

"What's the meaning of this? What gives you the right?"

The man, two inches taller than Papa, puts his camouflaged cap underneath his arm as he scouts the property then stands with his thick mustache, almost touching Papa's face. "Everything is explained in the document. We'll be back in a few days to collect the keys," the guard reprimands. The heavy smell of nicotine from his mouth consumes Papa, then the man turns around, and the G2s head towards the door.

"Come back here! You can't do this! This is my property! I built it, worked it, and grew it with my family!" he screams uselessly.

The men ignore his pleading and continue to walk out. Papa starts to charge at them in a fit of rage, but the employee grabs him by the arms to stop him. "Be careful! You don't know what they'll do," the employee pleads with him. Papa breathes heavily sweat pouring from his brow. He shakes his fist at their backs as they leave.

The guard with the cap turns around to see the commotion. "We'll be back in a few days!" he says with a smug grin.

Papa fumes as he stomps into the house. The employee follows him while Papa sits down to read the documents. Fidel has passed a law stating that all land and businesses are the property of the government. The government will pay Papa their assessed value of his empire.

"Look at this amount!" With fury, he waves the paper in front of the employee's face. "Our business is worth much more than that! Fidel is stealing my business!"

The employee tries to console him. He places a hand gently on his shoulder to calm him. "I know jefe, but what can we do?" the employee asks.

"Nothing!" Solemnly, he looks at his employee with empty eyes. Tears begin to stream uncontrollably down Papa's face. He doesn't bother to wipe them.

Mama comes in, sits next to him, and begins reading the document, her mouth wide open. All the blood, sweat and tears Papa put into all his fruits and coffee fincas, stores, gas stations, vehicles, boat, and homes now belong to Fidel, a man who never worked a single day on Papa's land.

A few days later, government men arrive. Papa stands behind the counter, eyes focused on the man, taking inventory. Two stocky men stand guard at the door, gripping their rifles, while a tall G2 roams the store. Papa glares at the drab olive uniform and shiny black boots. He is disgusted by this full bearded figure making its way towards him. The guard stands at the counter, with a notebook under his arm as he grips a cigar from his mouth and sneers. Papa stands behind the counter, with an employee standing guard.

"The keys," the guard demands with a hand extended.

Papa sullenly looks at his employee, who puts his hand on Papa's shoulder.

"Keys, now!" the guard yells.

Papa's hands shake as he hands them over. The guard grabs the notebook to register the keys for each property. He gives Papa his first check. With a pit in his stomach, he takes the meaningless piece of paper. The military men walk out with grins on their faces.

Papa stares at the check as if the number will increase with time. Consumed with grief, the pit in his stomach turns into stone as he blinks away his tears. In reality, they've stolen millions from him. He feels sick at the thought.

"What happens now, boss?" the employee asks.

"I don't know, friend," Papa responds consolingly.

"What will I do now? What will all of us do?"

Papa felt bewildered. His empire had been the lifeblood of the family. He didn't know who he was without it. "We'll figure something out. You are always welcome here. Mama and I will always help in any way we can."

All over the island, Cuban businesses are falling like Dominos into the hands of the government. Tension spreads like a web throughout the country. Some begin to live in fear as Cubans whisper the fate that follows anyone who defies the government.

A few weeks pass, and Papa sits at his dining room table writing his sons a letter. Papa worries about Cristian and Samuel in Havana. They have to be cautious when writing and sending letters. The censorship laws have become very rigid. The Fidel regime now intercepts the mail. Any derogatory comments of the government will lead to severe consequences.

16 – Article

*With the Mafia and Batista's men eliminated, Fidel
appoints himself prime minister, claiming Batista
abandoned Cuba. He takes charge of the army and assigns
a new cabinet. Manuel Urrutia, a lawyer, becomes Interim
President. Fidel appoints his brother Raul to Minister of
Defense and his friend Che Guevara as Head of the Central
Bank.*

*It is July of 1959 when the interim president
becomes suspicious. He fears Fidel plans to reform the
government and resigns. On live TV, Urrutia opposes
business with the Russians.*

1959

In Havana, the brothers rest in their room. Cristian
sits by the window shining his shoes with a pressed suit
hanging on a hook behind him. He peeks out the window,
admiring the crowd of pedestrians. Addicted to the busy
city life, he is anxious to go out for the night. Samuel sits
on his bed, reading the paper. His thick eyebrows tip down
as he digests the article.

"This is ridiculous. Look at this," Samuel shows Cristian an article in the paper. The headline quotes Fidel, "The Revolution is as Green as Our Palm Trees." "He expects us to believe that he's not red like the Communist flag!" Samuel shouts.

"He's trying to kill rumors that he's a Communist," Cristian frowns. "Who does he think he's fooling?"

"He's a Communist, a criminal, and a thief! This is pissing me off! First our business, now this."

"I know. I could hear the pain in Papa's voice when I read his letter. He worked so hard. All the long hours, sweat, days away from home, then this dictator comes along and takes it all!" Cristian slams his shoeshine brush on the table.

"He better step down, bring back elections, and give everything back. This crap has gone on long enough!"

"What the hell is he really trying to prove?"

"We have to do something! This can't happen again. We didn't risk our lives, watch our friend die, just to have another take over!" His mind flashes back to his friend Carlos, a young man who did not get to live a full life. Their last time together, the two shared their dreams. Samuel confessed he would leave the family business, joining Cristian in Havana to pursue an engineering career.

Carlos also planned to move to the city to start his own accounting business. He clears his throat. "Tonight, we'll come up with a plan," Samuel continues. "We're meeting with a good group of people."

"Don't worry, Samuel. We'll get this idiot out of here, just like the last one."

The brothers get dressed and head downstairs. They pause, startled by the crowd gathered in the lobby, and notice the residents' eyes glued to the television. A man yells, "What the hell is this! He's lost his mind."

"What's going on?" Samuel asks the receptionist.

"Fidel has been on Tele Mundo for hours lashing out at Urrutia and threatening to resign due to Urrutia's opposition."

"Good, I hope he resigns!" Cristian pats Samuel on the back. "See, I told you he would be out of here soon."

"Let's finish watching this at our meeting," Samuel tells Cristian. "Maybe this will all be over tonight."

At a rebel's house, the brothers meet with a group of university students and professors. They chat and laugh while sipping their Malta drinks, as smoke from their cigars and cigarettes fill the air.

"Okay," the owner of the house announces. "I know we're ready for tonight, but before we leave, we need to figure out a way to increase our propaganda."

"I bought printing paper and found a new printing press," Samuel announces. "It's at the warehouse. Cristian will go over there tomorrow to fix it." Cristian nods.

"Thank you guys," the rebel responds, "for your generosity and patriotism."

The group agrees, thanking the brothers. A professor pats Samuel on the back. "We'll get the truth out to the rest of the island, and everyone will join us to get this communist out of here." The men all nod in agreement.

The meeting adjourns, and the brothers head to meet their dates. At the theater, ladies in their designer dresses and hats hold hands with their partners in their black suits. Samuel's date adjusts her white gloves, as Cristian's friend digs in her purse. The crowd makes their way into the theater and the brothers part ways to their seats. Cristian sits with his partner in a balcony at the north end, while Samuel picks seats in the center. Other rebels place themselves at separate balconies.

The audience enjoys the entertainment, showing their approval with applause at the intermission when the ladies search in their purses for flyers. Lights go out, announcing the pause before the second act, then the brothers, their dates, and the other rebels release the pamphlets. A shower of leaflets lands on the first floor distracting spectators as lights come back. Guards in the theater read the announcements:

> *"400,000 political prisoners, 20,000 assassinations.*
> *These amounts constitute the love and cordiality*
> *among Cubans.*
> *José Martí"*

"Out, everybody out of the theater," a guard announces.

G2s and military cars, greet the crowd as they step out of the theater. Guards weed out suspects, directing couples to move along while shoving single men and women into cars. Cristian and Samuel walk away with their dates, pleased with their efforts.

17 – Office

Fidel stays in office. Dreading retaliation, Urrutia flees to the embassy. Fearing for his life, he leaves the island. Fidel summons his men to capture Urrutia at the embassy, but they are too late.

One evening, Cubans decide to send a clear message. They deposit bombs in electricity offices, public offices, and the Shell refinery. Explosions and fires alert the authorities. The next morning employees show up to work only to find shutdown companies. The new revolution disrupts Fidel's businesses while ensuring civilians are safe.

1959

A couple of days after the bombings, Cristian sits at the back of a bus. He looks out the window watching a couple walk hand in hand when he hears a whistle. His eyes shift down the street to a man waving at a group that stands by a crowded café. Cristian grabs the stack of flyers in his briefcase and lets them fly out the window, as he watches pedestrians catch and pick up the pieces of paper. He taps his foot as the bus continues on the route. At the next stop, he jumps out of his seat and shoves his way through a couple of passengers. His heart beats while he serpentines through the crowd of pedestrians, continuing on his walk for several blocks relieved that no one has followed him. He makes a right turn at the corner and slows down his pace when he is tapped on the shoulder. Startled and with wide eyes, he turns around.

An hour later, Cristian storms into their room. Out of breath, he tells Samuel, "Good, you're here!" He bends over with his hands on his knees.

Samuel puts his pen and paper down, "What's wrong?"

"Fidel is retaliating after the attacks a couple of nights ago."

"How do you know?"

"I was distributing flyers, and a friend pulled me into an alley," Cristian responds as he sits on his bed to catch his breath. "He told me to get home, be careful, and lay low for a day or two."

"Why? What happened?"

"They are arresting people to scare anyone that is rebelling."

Samuel is furious that they have to hide like fugitives. He fidgets around their room anxious to get back out and get this dictator out of their country. Cristian observes his anxious brother and worries if he will do something reckless.

Another week passes. In Havana, Samuel and Cristian casually walk down the street on their way to the Malecón, the boardwalk near the Parque de Trillo. Pedestrians fill the Malecón as sea waves crash against the stone wall on this breezy evening. The brothers inch along the curb to avoid getting splashed. Samuel waves to acquaintances as Cristian gazes out at the sea. Cristian's long strides distance him from Samuel. He pauses when he realizes Samuel is no longer next to him. Crowds lounge on the wall benches as Cristian looks around for his brother. Along the monument of the USS Maine, a memorial to the sunken battleship, a crowd gathers, where Cristian spots Samuel in the middle of the group. He shakes his head, annoyed and approaches the crowd. Their entire life, Cristian has had to wait for his little brother to finish being the center of attention.

In the crowd, ladies look at Samuel with star-struck eyes. Men listen to him as if he's the Pope. *Papa is right,* Cristian thinks to himself, *Samuel will be a politician someday.* Cristian puts his hand on his shoulder.

"Sorry, hermano," Samuel says as he turns around spotting Cristian. "Everyone, this is my brother, Cristian." The group salutes him.

"We have to get to the office," Cristian says. The "office" is code for a rebel meeting. Any rebels in the group would understand the importance of them leaving. Non-rebels would assume they had to get to work.

Samuel looks at his watch. "Oh, man! We're going to be late," he tells the others. "I'll catch up with you guys later."

"Were you working on your campaign speech?" Cristian teases Samuel as they walk away.

"Shut up!" Samuel shoves him. "We're meeting my friend, Roberto, tonight. You remember him from Imias?"

"Yeah, he's a good guy."

"Now, he's president of this region's Federation of Students. He said he needs our help."

"What do we need to do?"

"We'll be helping in any capacity necessary. In the beginning, it'll be running errands."

"That's fine. Whatever it takes to get our country back."

Several minutes have passed, it's after business hours when the brothers arrive at a bank.

"Go, I'll block you," Cristian tells Samuel, "No one is watching."

Samuel takes a toothpick out of his pocket, jamming it in the lock of the door. "Let's go," he tells Cristian.

Several blocks down, they stop at a government office building. "Cover me," Cristian tells Samuel. The men continue on the walk to their destination.

18 – Coordinator

Raul Castro and others meet with Communist party leaders. October of 1959, Huber Matos, Fidel's head military commander, writes a letter to Fidel stating his disagreement with his actions and resigns. Raul wants him executed, but Fidel does not want a martyr and sends him to prison in isolation for 20 years. Others in his party resign in protest, leave for the US, or begin a new revolutionary movement to overthrow Fidel.

Fidel is viewed as a savior by some but feared to be a Communist by others. Rumors circulate that his brother, Raul, and others in his government are also Communists. The United States urges Fidel to hold public elections. Fidel claims that people do not want public elections because elections in the past only brought turmoil.

1959

Cristian and Samuel arrive at their friend's house.

"Welcome my brothers!" Roberto greets them.

"Thank you, mi hermano," Samuel hugs him, patting his back. "You remember my brother Cristian."

"Great to see you again," Cristian shakes his hand.

"Join us. Have a seat, and we'll get started."
Cristian and Samuel pull up chairs to the dining room table, surrounded by fellow rebels.

"How did everyone's mission go?" Roberto asks.

"We got our targets," Samuel responds, "Those communist workers won't be able to get into work tomorrow."

Another rebel states, "I wish I could see their faces when they can't get their dirty work done."

"Fidel will be fuming with all the money he loses," Roberto says with a chuckle.

The rebels' discussion starts lighthearted but quickly intensifies as the men vent about the tyrant.

"Gentlemen, there have been several alarming turns of events," Roberto says. "We are all very familiar with Huber Matos. He fought alongside Fidel against Batista. A noble and brave soldier."

"An honest rebel. Everyone knows Matos," another man announces.

"His resignation is very disturbing," Roberto responds. The group mumbles disagreements. "Matos wrote Fidel a letter letting him know he was well aware of Fidel's army distributing Marxist propaganda."

"Finally, we get the truth," Samuel states.

"It's disturbing," Roberto continues. "In the letter, Matos states his disagreement with the Agrarian Reform, Fidel's response to Urrutia's resignation, Marxist propaganda, communist rumors, and other actions."

"First Urrutia, now Matos. Who will be next?" Samuel says.

"Hopefully, Fidel!" another man says.

"It gets worse," Roberto, continues. "Fidel sent Camilo Cienfuegos to arrest Matos. He told Camilo that Matos was starting a revolution."

"That bastard!" Samuel shouts. "Everyone knows Camilo and Matos are great friends."

"Fidel claims Camilo is his right-hand man and the only one to do the job," Roberto says. "Rumor has it that Camilo called Fidel and told him Huber was just resigning. Camilo headed back home on a small plane, which has now mysteriously disappeared." The room fell silent.

"We all know what happened," Samuel responds. "Fidel is behind all of it. He is up to no good!"

"Now Matos is behind bars," a man says.

"For speaking his mind, and stepping down," Samuel speaks. "It's unjust to arrest someone for speaking or turning down a job! Fidel is turning out to be just as bad, if not worse, than Batista."

"People are upset about Matos' arrest," Roberto continues. "We need to pull all our resources, recruit as many as possible to get rid of this Diablo!"

"Count me in! What do you need?" Samuel volunteers. "He tricked us into getting rid of the murderer before him only to make way for his malicious plans with his minions, his vicious brother, and crooked friend!"

"Fidel used us during the revolution and made us his puppets!" a man shouts.

"I'm not going to let him get away with this!" Samuel continues. "I will fight until the day we have a truly democratic government and free elections!"

"Amen brother!" several men roar.

"We need to get him where it hurts," Roberto comments. "He wants power and money. So, we'll sabotage all his businesses."

"How soon can we get started?" Samuel asks.

The group discusses other organizations' plans for a revolution. Roberto delegates assignments to members in the room. Cristian and Samuel are very well aware of the danger, and as a precaution, they now have aliases. This new revolution consumes their time, not allowing much room for studies. The brothers keep their new identities a secret from Papa. They make a pact that they will return to their studies when Fidel is overthrown.

Samuel begins his involvement by raising funds for the finance group. The money will trickle down to support other agendas, primarily raising funds for arsenal. Preparations are underway by the military group in case of a battle. Additional funds help families of political prisoners or those killed, as well as members in hiding.

Cristian assists the propaganda group with advertising. The underground newspaper, Patria Libre Estudantil, keeps the public informed of new developments about the government and ways to help with the revolution. Sabotaging and damaging Fidel's properties becomes the priority for the new revolution.

One rainy afternoon, they head to a restaurant for another meeting. Running down the sidewalk, they dodge puddles while holding newspapers over their heads to shelter themselves from the downpour. As they step into the restaurant, the bartender salutes them with a nod. Then he pours rum in a glass of Coke for a customer. Several men gather at the bar in deep conversations, while a couple laughs at a table. Samuel spots their group at the back of the restaurant. Five men sit around a table with beers and

Cuba Libres, rum and Cokes. One of them waves Samuel and Cristian over.

The men discuss new plans. Samuel's magnetic and positive attitude prompts changes in their assigned roles.

"What happens now that they've elected you coordinator of our student group?" Cristian questions Samuel.

"I have to go undercover," Samuel informs him. "Will you be my right-hand man?"

"I would be your right-hand man whether you asked or not."

"We're moving to a new guesthouse. I'll have to go to another location. You'll be the only one that will know where to find me."

"I better know your every move. You do nothing until you tell me. Got it?"

"Don't worry. I'll be fine, and we'll get this bastard out of our land!"

The group elects Samuel as the head of the Student Sector in Havana University. Fidel continually seeks the leaders of rebel groups to incarcerate, torture, or send to the firing squad.

19 – Piece of Paper

1960 arrives with no change in sight. A Soviet politician visits Cuba. The Castros and the Soviet official wine, dine, and smoke cigars. Fidel and his guest shake hands to make trade agreements. Concerns grow on the island over the new Russian friendship and plans for the arrival of Soviet weapons. Cuba swarms with suspicion of a Communist government takeover as Fidel begins to receive assistance from the Soviet Union. Citizens fear a new dictator has risen.

Groups spring up in secrecy throughout the island with members from all walks of life; university students, doctors, lawyers, business professionals, and many others. Rebels who fought alongside Fidel, now find themselves fighting against him. On live TV, Fidel demands "Elections for what?"

1960

One afternoon, Cristian and Samuel return to the Malecón. Cadillac's, Chryslers, and convertibles buzz by as the horn of a bus sounds to avoid a near collision. Grey clouds roll in over the horizon as Cristian and Samuel walk the streets.

The brothers lean on the wall to admire the deep blue sea. They hope to blend in as tourists rather than rebels of the revolution. The men are meeting another student to retrieve a message from a different group. Samuel has met with her before. Cristian accompanies him to learn the procedure for future messages. At their destination, they rest against the half wall causally, trying not to arouse suspicion.

"Have you responded to Papa's letter?" Samuel asks.

"No," Cristian responds. "I don't know what to say. He is still in mourning about his business. I can't drop another bomb on him."

"You aren't doing anything wrong."

"I know, but it feels like it. Papa expects this behavior from you."

"Hey!"

"It's true. You have always been rebellious. Nothing wrong with that, but I have always done as Papa says. It'll break his heart."

"Alejandro and Alberto are there."

"I know, but he wanted all of us to take care of the business. Now I'm going to tell him that I'm doing my own thing."

"When this is over and Papa gets his properties back, he is going to be so busy. Our brothers and all his employees will be there to help him, and he won't even miss you."

In the distance, Cristian spots a rather distinguished, tall, slender, strawberry blonde. She captivates him and he cannot take his eyes off her. She walks in their direction.

"Did you hear me?" Samuel slaps Cristian on the arm.

"What?" Cristian replies, looking at Samuel with star-struck eyes.

"What's wrong with you?"

"Sorry, I was distracted by that gorgeous creature!" Cristian responds as he guides his eyes in her direction.

"Oh, that's Cecilia."

She walks up to them, giving Samuel a warm embrace.

"Hi Cecilia, this is my brother Cristian," Samuel makes the introductions.

"Hello, Cecilia," Cristian's heart races. "Very nice to meet you." His mouth feels dry. He starts to fiddle with his shirt to make sure that he is presentable.

"Nice to meet you too," she responds, with a brief handshake.

Cecilia quickly settles her attention on Samuel. Disappointed by her reaction, Cristian ponders what he can say or do to get a reaction out of her.

Their conversation quickly turns into topics of the revolution. She gets fired up when talking about the cause. Her spitfire personality fascinates and intrigues Cristian.

"Are you comfortable accompanying our friend to the drop?" Samuel checks with Cecilia.

"Of course. Whatever it takes to get this Communist off our island!" Cecilia retorts.

"It's dangerous. Are you sure you're okay doing this?" Cristian worries.

"I'll be fine. Don't worry about me; just make sure your friend does his part!" Cecilia says confidently.

She discreetly reaches in her purse to take out a folded piece of paper. She shakes Samuel's hand to transfer the hidden document. Samuel takes the message as she says goodbye, disappearing into the crowd.

That evening, Cecilia walks into a club with a group of rebels. Couples Mambo on the dance floor, while others drink and talk at the bar. As customers socialize and dance, Cecilia's friends take small, round objects out of their pockets, throwing them in as they walk by plants and garbage cans. Smoke fills the room and bodies stampede out the door. Throughout the city, other rebels fill movie theaters and restaurants with smoke, causing Fidel's businesses to close for the night.

20 – Rendezvous

One night in April of 1961, the last customer leaves as employees turn off the lights at the El Encanto, a major department store. A group sneaks behind the store setting the building on fire. The blaze puts a small damper in Fidel's economy. Fidel captures the rebels and commands his guards to assassinate some as an example to others.

Advertisements in clandestine rebel newspapers recruit men and women. Cubans cautiously enlist friends and acquaintances. Many members have aliases and are careful of whom they allow in their circle, as G2s are infiltrating the groups.

1961

A few weeks later, Samuel and Cristian get ready to go out. Cristian puts on his newly shined shoes. Samuel brushes lint off his suit.

"Here you go." Cristian hands Samuel his gun.

"Thanks," Samuel says, tucking the weapon in his back, adjusting it between his pants, then letting his jacket cover it up. "We're meeting the girls at the café."

"I'll be several steps behind you with my date, keeping an eye on you."

"Don't worry about me. The two of us will be fine."

"So, what's going on with you two?" Cristian inquires.

"Nothing, we're both focused on this cause. Quit hounding me," Samuel punches Cristian in the arm. "Remember, at 5:10, everything goes off, so you better make sure no one is around and you two are out of the building."

"Got it."

The men head out to the street. A small crowd gathers at the corner as the bus pulls up. They stroll window-shopping to keep G2s off their trail. The brothers walk by a store with a line of angry customers waiting.

"Look at this!" Samuel points to the line. "Can you believe what Fidel is doing?"

"I can't believe he's even rationing the meat!" Cristian responds. "Remember how we used to be able to buy anything we wanted?" he says in a nostalgic tone.

"Yeah, especially in our store. Papa would get Mama anything she needed to make dinner. Now, he must

wait in these ridiculous lines to put food on the table."
Infuriated, Samuel yells, "This is ridiculous!"

Cristian yanks him by the arm, leading him away
from the store, "Quiet! You're going to draw attention to
us."

Samuel jerks away from his brother.

"Come on, let's go. The girls are waiting. Let's get
this done," Cristian says.

At the café, the ladies wait in the outdoor seating
area. They greet each other with kisses on the cheeks.

"We'll meet at the rendezvous at 5:30," Samuel
informs the group.

"We'll be behind you until you get to the theater,"
Cristian alerts him.

"Have a good time, you two," Samuel jokes as he
grabs Clara's hand, then walks off.

"It's a nice night," Cristian says to Maria, lifting
his arm,

"Yes it is," she responds, putting her arm
underneath his. They begin their walk, keeping a distance
from Samuel. Cristian keeps an eye on his little brother
until Samuel heads into the theater.

"Two, please," Samuel asks the attendant at the
ticket booth.

He takes the money, "Here you go, sir. Enjoy the show." The couple heads in to wait in the seating line.

Cristian turns around to make sure his brother is safe as they walk. Several doors down from the theater, they arrive at the restaurant. He wipes his sweaty hands on his pants before opening the door. They head to the bar. "Cola, please," Cristian asks the bartender.

"Five cents," the bartender requests.

"Thank you." The couple shares the drink.

In the restaurant, at 5:05, Cristian shows Maria his watch. She gets up, brushes lint off her dress, claps her purse and heads to the ladies' room. She checks the stalls and with an empty restroom, she rests her purse on the counter. Slowly she puts her hand in her purse, pausing when touching the bomb, and the reality of what will happen sinks in. She takes several deep breaths and composes herself. There is no going back now.

At the same time, in the bathroom at the theater, Clara touches up her lipstick as she waits for an older woman to leave.

"Enjoy the show," Clara tells the elderly woman.

"Thank you, you too," she responds as she walks out.

Clara combs her hair, then looks at her watch. With confidence and pride of her role in the revolution, she reaches for the bomb.

The rebels pull the homemade bombs, with watches, out of their purses. Carefully placing them in the garbage cans, the women leave the bathrooms to join their dates.

In the cinema, the line at the foyer moves into the theater as Samuel and Clara leave the building.

At the restaurant, a female heads towards the bathroom. "They are cleaning the bathroom," Maria's heart races as she stops a woman. "You'll have to wait a few minutes until they come out."

At 5:09, Cristian takes the last gulp from the glass. He grabs Maria's hand, and they leave the restaurant.

Within minutes, blasts fill business bathrooms and closets with smoke. The shockwaves ignite panic and chaos. Debris flies into the air. The streets are flooded with sounds of coughing and loud screams. The rebels feel their plan has been successful.

21 – Civilian

Fidel states in an interview that he does not torture, assassinate, or have political prisoners. The Cuban economy begins to suffer. Fidel imposes meat rations, allowing only the purchase of several pounds of meat per person per month.

It's April 17, 1961, when a group of Cuban exiles, with the aid of the CIA, disembarks on Playa Girón to attack la Bahía de Cochinos, the Bay of Pigs. With weapons loaded, they quietly sneak onto land. In the fields, an ambush waits for the exiles and captures them. Fidel, aware of the plan, ruins President Kennedy's attempt to overthrow the regime.

1961

That night, Cristian is working the late shift when the military storms in. The government holds employees hostage. They are determined to find rebels connected to the Bay of Pigs invasion.

The next morning G2s bang on Samuel's door. "Open up!"

"Who is it?" Samuel asks.

"The military. Open up now!"

Samuel opens the door as soldiers storm in. He steps back to avoid the pack of G2s, tripping and knocking over a chair. Two men shove Samuel against the wall, handcuffing him. They race him down the stairs, then push him into the back seat of a black car waiting outside. Samuel sits quietly, sandwiched between two guards. Rebels have reported beatings on car rides if they fight or protest. His mind races with thoughts and questions. *Do they know he was part of the sabotage on businesses?* They made sure the coast was clear. No one was hurt, except Fidel's pocketbook. He thinks to himself. *If they know I was there, they might know about the girls and Cristian. Were they caught too? Are they ok?* His thoughts distract him and he loses track of time.

In a penitentiary, a herd of men packs a cell. Some lay on the narrow, iron-framed bunk beds, while others chat. A few men glance at the entrance when guards shove Samuel in, and he stumbles. Ready to turn around throwing punches, he pauses. He inhales picturing Carlos. Mama's face flashes before him. He composes himself and begins to roam the room, observing and saluting many familiar faces. A man sits against the wall with his head down. Another kneels praying, while several men gather around a bunk bed talking. One of them flails his arms, cursing. Against a wall, Samuel sees Juan, a face he knows. He joins Juan and a couple others.

In another part of town, a taxi driver returns home from work. G2s pull up in a truck behind him and the men in the truck demand the citizen to stop. He turns around to face guns. In the street, neighbors run for cover. An official pulls him by the arm.

"Let me go!" the man yells. "What the hell's going on?"

Another military man appears, and they throw him in the back of a truck, punching, and kicking. "Shut up and get in!" they command.

The truck arrives at the prison. Guards throw the man in a cell. He wanders the room, scanning thousands of faces when Juan recognizes Felipe and flags him over. "Why are you in here?" the rebel asked the man.

"I don't know!" Felipe responds. "I ran out to pick up medicine for my son. I had just gotten home from the pharmacy when they pulled up. They dragged me here with no explanation."

"That's terrible amigo," Juan responds.

"My family must be worried out of their mind. I didn't get to give my son his medicine," Felipe continues.

"Those bastards," Juan fumes. "What the hell is going on."

"They can't just arrest people with no cause," Samuel says. "Look at all of us. We can retaliate and start a coup."

"Then what? They have guns. We wouldn't stand a chance!" Juan responds.

"You're right. I'm just so damn furious right now. We have to figure something out. Join us, amigo," Samuel suggests to Felipe.

"Felipe, this is Samuel," Juan makes the introductions. "He's a good friend of mine."

Several minutes pass before the guards walk in, dragging Felipe out.

"What will they do to him?" Juan asks another inmate. He knows Felipe is an innocent civilian and knows nothing. "I fear for him, my friend!"

Later two guards march in, walking up to Samuel.

"Let's go," one G2 commands.

"Where am I going?" Samuel asks.

"I said let's go!" The guards grab him by the arms, dragging him through the cell.

Samuel decides to stay silent in hopes to avoid beatings. He tries to walk, but his feet drag with the guards' tight grip and quick steps. They haul him down a dim corridor and into an interrogation room, shoving him onto a chair with his hands tied as a big bright light rests on his head. The men circle him in the chair. Samuel sweats profusely. He can't swallow and feels flushed with fear.

"Why weren't you at work!" a guard with a thick beard yells in his face.

"Because he was busy planning the Bay of Pigs attack," the other guard slaps Samuel on the head.

"What!" Samuel yells. "What the hell are you talking about?"

"We know you and all your friends concocted this invasion," the bushy bearded guard states. "Tell us who was involved and in charge and we'll let you go."

"He was in charge!" the other guard growls, slapping Samuel again.

"Stop hitting me!" Samuel barks, "I was home sick." Samuel realizes he is being falsely accused. *What are they talking about?* His fear turns to anger.

"Were you in charge of this cowardly act?" the bearded guard yells at Samuel.

"I told you I was home, sick!" Samuel fires back.

"Sure, you were. You were hiding, you coward. You knew all about this!"

"I don't know what the hell you're talking about."

A punch in the face almost knocks Samuel out of his seat. "You're the coward. Beating me up with my hands tied. For no reason!" Another punch in the face.

"Shut up!"

"You have nothing on me. I've done nothing wrong."

"Put him in the dungeon!" the furious guard commands to the others. "A few hours in there, then he'll talk."

They drag and throw Samuel into a dark, cold room. He feels around. The cold concrete walls make him quiver. Claustrophobia sinks in as he realizes he's in tight quarters. His heart races and he struggles to breathe. *Get it together. You'll get out of this*, he thinks to himself.

"Hello," he calls out, checking if he's alone.

He sits down to let his eyes adjust. As he slowly moves his hand across the ground near him, he feels a hole. A foul stench seeps from it as he realizes it's sewage and crawls away from it. For hours, he sits in a fetal position, shivering uncontrollably. He wiggles his extremities, hoping the pain from the punches will subside, as thoughts of dying from hypothermia race through his mind. Finally, they return for more beatings and questioning. Samuel remains a vault. The frustrated guards throw him back in the cell with the others.

Several hours earlier, a guard walks into the cell, and with a firm grip, grabs hold of Juan's arm, dragging him out.

"What's going on? Why am I here?" Juan yells as they punch, shove, and kick him down the dark corridor.

The abuse subsides as a military man shoves him into a small concrete room. A chair and a bright light above it are the only items in the interrogation room. Powerful and unexpected punches knock the rebel to the ground. The beating continues, with Juan bouncing off the wall.

"Who planned the attacks?" military men yell. "What is your next move? Who helped you?"

"I don't know what you're talking about," the weakened man responds.

The guards drag him to another room, strapping him to a chair. An injection penetrates his skin to force out the truth. As an allergic reaction begins to suffocate him, they abandon Juan to suffer and consider confessing. Juan gasps for air; images of his mom and sister flood his mind. *He can't die now; they all have to fight.* He thinks to himself. Pictures of his time on the mountains strengthen his will to live. *We can win this fight*, he tells himself. His breathing settles down as he starts to doze off. When they return, the beatings continue. Despite hours of torture, he still refuses to speak. Finally, half dead, they throw him back into the cell like discarded trash.

Samuel sees his weak, almost unconscious friend and goes by his side.

"I got you, brother," Samuel assures Juan. "You'll be ok."

22 – Apartment

The rebel groups on the island are oblivious to the Bay of Pigs plot, but Fidel suspects they led the attack and sends out a massive search party for rebels.

Fidel's informants obtain lists of anyone who did not show up for work to arrest them. Guards search homes and businesses for evidence. All suspicious items will land individuals in the penitentiary, and innocent Cubans go into custody. Many are contained in a stadium when the prisons overflow.

1961

Samuel nurses Juan back to health as his friend relives the torture he endured.

"They forced me to stand on a stool with a noose around my neck, demanding I speak or the stool would be gone," Juan recalls in horror.

"Oh my brother, I'm so sorry you had to endure that." Samuel rips off the pocket from his own shirt and dips it in a small cup of water. "What did you do?"

"I tipped the stool out from underneath me," Juan manages to force a small grin. "They are not going to get anything out of me."

"You lunatic," Samuel teases him as he rings the cloth over the cup. "You're a true patriot." He dabs the damp cloth on the gash on Juan's forehead.

"They were messing with my mind. The noose wasn't fastened to anything. I fell to the ground."

"Those bastards!"

"My defiance infuriated the guards. They dragged me to a big tank of water in the corner to dunk me in and out of it. I was sure that they'd leave me there to drown."

"What did they want?"

"They kept asking me who organized the Bay of Pigs attack. Hell, I didn't even know that was going to happen. Did you?"

"No. No one in my group said anything about it."

"It was hard, brother. I thought I was going to die."

The next afternoon, after the Bay of Pigs, Cristian is allowed to leave work, heading straight to his brother's apartment.

Cristian reaches the street of Samuel's home. He climbs the hill with urgency to check on his brother. An eerie silence fills the block. People hide after the recent events. As he steps into the building, a sense of panic consumes him. Before he reaches the flight of stairs, the receptionist stops him.

"They took him this morning!" she informs Cristian.

Frozen with terror, he manages to choke out, "What happened?"

"He stayed home sick yesterday," she explains. "Someone at the post office must have told the military. They charged in and took him! It all happened so quickly. Nobody could stop them."

Cristian does not know where to find Samuel. Frantic, he goes back to work.

"Can I take a few days to find my brother?" Cristian pleads with his boss.

"I need you here! We have a lot of work," his boss roars indifferent to his suffering.

"I have to go and find him!"

"If you leave, don't come back!"

"So be it!" Cristian storms out to begin his desperate search. He meets up with Pablo, a longtime friend and rebel. Pablo, a short, stocky man, seeks his girlfriend, also taken into custody. They stop at all the prisons, with no luck. Cristian walks home with his head down, oblivious to his surroundings, and bumps into a woman who drops her bag. A pineapple and oranges roll out.

"Excuse me," Cristian pleads.

"Watch where you're walking," she responds.

Cristian helps her pick up the fruit and continues home. *What am I going to tell Papa? He pictures Papa fuming and Mama hysterical. He will find Samuel and they will never find out.* He spends the night restlessly planning his next steps.

23 - The Holy Grail

There is an exodus of families affected by the Agrarian Reform. Some gather as many personal belongings as possible, fearing that otherwise their belongings will be taken away. Others leave with as little as possible, afraid of being caught. Many stay thinking things will change soon.

Fidel cancels Christmas. Newspapers report on the weak economy and the communist agenda. Fidel shuts down or takes over radio stations and TV channels.

1961

Cristian spends the next couple of days meeting with rebels to see if anyone has news. One day, on his way home, a friend stops him on the street.

"I was looking for my roommate at the prison," he informs Cristian, "and saw Samuel's name on the list."

"Thank you, brother!" Overjoyed, he finds Pablo, who had managed to locate his girlfriend, and the two men dash over to the prison.

Family and friends, eager to see their loved ones, wait in line. Cristian finally gets up to the counter to give them Samuel's name. The guard runs his finger down a list of names.

With an insolent tone in his voice, he says, "That man is not at this location."

"He was just here," he shouts. "Where did you take him?" Cristian slams his hand on the counter.

"Settle down, Cristian," Pablo pats him on the back. "They'll throw you behind bars, too."

The government finally divulges the new location, with no explanation of why they moved Samuel. Cristian arrives at an abandoned prison, reopened to house the large number of detainees after the Bay of Pigs. When he enters, guards do not allow him to see Samuel. Cristian steps out, rubbing his head. He wants to scream and punch a wall or the guard, and burst in to free his brother. He pauses and breaths. *Be rational*, he thinks to himself. Defeated, he returns home.

Outside Cristian's apartment building, Pablo leans on the wall, smoking a cigarette as he waits for Cristian to arrive. Cristian sees him, and the men pat each other on the back.

"I'm so glad to see you, brother," Cristian somberly announces.

"I was hoping to see both of you strolling up the hill," Pablo says.

"I feel like I'm in search of the Holy Grail. First, they move him, and then they won't let me see him. I have to wait a few more days before I can visit him. They'll probably move him again before my scheduled day."

"They're playing games with you. They have done this to other families, moving men and women from one prison to another, to make their families think their loved ones have disappeared."

"What a sick and demented game! Now I have to sit here and wait until they tell me when I can see him."

"I'm here for you. Let me know what you need."

"Thank you!" Cristian passes his days in agony, not knowing his little brother's condition.

At the prison, days go by in the cold, concrete cell. A light stays on to confuse prisoners about the time of day. Rats and cockroaches crawl out of the hole in the ground that serves as the prisoners' toilet. A faucet sits next to the hole for additional water. Prisoners survive on sugared water and plain bread for breakfast, with lunch and dinner consisting of bland, watered down beans, bread, plain spaghetti or corn. Allotted only four cups of water a day, the men conserve some water to wash up. Deprived of covers, the men tremble in the cold cells at night.

One day at dawn, the guards drag Samuel out of his cell, wanting him sleep deprived, hoping for a confession. Samuel stands by the wall, wondering what is next. Guards point their guns, and Samuel thinks of Cristian roaming the streets looking for him, and Papa, oblivious to what his sons have been doing. Suddenly, guns go off. Samuel's ears ring from the blasts. His body slams against the wall. Sharp pain ripples through his arms and torso. Realizing he is still standing and the guards are shooting blanks, he endures the pain, grateful that he is not dead. The guards continue to pry for answers.

Samuel cries out, "I don't know anything!"

Once again, guards drag him through the corridor. Fed up and not caring what happens, Samuel is ready to start throwing punches. *I will go down with a fight*, he thinks to himself. Suddenly, the guards throw him outside.

That afternoon, Cristian sits on his bed, reading a paper. A jiggle on the doorknob spooks him. Slowly, the bedroom door swings open, startling him. A worn down, disheveled, bruised, and tired figure steps in. Overcome with relief; he jumps up to embrace Samuel.

"They finally let me go when they couldn't get information out of me," Samuel utters, walking to Cristian's bed. "I just need to get some sleep," he continues, as he collapses on the bed.

Cristian takes his brother's shoes off, lifts his legs to adjust his body onto the bed. He covers Samuel with the blanket to let him rest, grateful that his brother has returned, and wondering what his brother endured these last few days. After Samuel catches up on his sleep, Cristian will probe him for answers.

Later that evening, Samuel fills Cristian in on his ordeal.

"I'm glad you're back! I've been frantically looking for you," Cristian explains his efforts to find him.

"You wouldn't believe what goes on in those Communist playpens. The other men shared their experiences with me."

"What did they say?"

"Prisoners were injected, causing pain and confusion. Others were dunked repeatedly to the point of almost drowning."

"That's barbaric! What's wrong with these people?"

"They're out of control. The government also threatened to arrest family members if they didn't talk. I know many lost their lives. The tortures were too much. Half the people they took were not even involved in the revolution."

"This government has to be stopped, Samuel."

"We will put an end to this! You'll see. Things will be back to normal soon."

"Juan stopped by while you were resting."

"He got out, thank God!"

"He said the guards just let him go, too." Cristian pauses as he responds. He sits down sighing, "He wanted me to let you know Felipe didn't make it. His family received notice that he was a traitor and sent to the firing squad."

"What! An innocent man, no trial, no jail time, just straight to the wall! God-damn-it!" Samuel kicks a chair. "Innocent people are dying. This has to stop! We have to help put an end to this!"

24 – Church

*Fidel publicly announces he is a Marxist. The
United States sees Fidel's true colors. Fidel's alliance with
the Soviet Union threatens the safety and peace of North,
Central, and South America. He makes his Communist
agenda clear, killing Cubans' hope for a democratic
government. Plans begin on a battle to overthrow this new
dictator. Fidel attacks religion, closing Catholic churches.*

1961

It's September 1961, time for the annual Saint
Caridad procession. A large crowd gathers outside the
church, Nuestra Senora de la Caridad del Cobre, where
parishioners commiserate, holding their Bibles and rosaries.

Cecilia walks up looking for her best friend, Maria.
Her green dress sways in the light breeze. She smiles,
saluting other church members while pulling a rosary out of
her purse. By the stairs, she spots Maria, a short, brown-
haired woman in a red skirt suit. Maria's eyes hide behind
sunglasses as she smiles and waves at Cecilia. As Cecilia
strolls to her friend, she notices a couple of military men
walking towards the church. She pauses as the guards

march in front of her, heading towards the steps of the church.

"What do you think they want?" Cecilia asks Maria.

"I don't know," Maria responds. "Should we ask that other guard? He has been here the whole time."

"Don't bother. He'll either ignore you or take you into custody."

"Where are the other girls?"

"I haven't seen them yet. I'm sure they'll get here soon."

A commotion at the church entrance stops their conversation.

"You can't stop the procession!" the priest whispers.

"By order of the government, this procession is canceled!" the G2 announces.

The crowd looks around, confused. The guard in the group rushes up the steps.

"What's going on?" he asks the military men.

"This event is canceled," a military man announces. "Help us get this crowd to disperse."

"This is nonsense! You can't stop this procession. It's an annual event. It's our time of worship. This is our right!" The guard stares down the G2.

"You better stand down and do as you're told, soldier!" the other military man demands.

"Absolutely not!" The guard takes off his holster and throws it on the ground. "This is a Holy place! You can't do this!"

Several parishioners climb up the stairs to calm down the guard.

"Let's go, friend," a man tells the guard. "You're going to get yourself killed."

"No! This has gone far enough!"

"Let's go!" Two other men join and escort the guard down the stairs.

The men manage to calm down the guard. A group surrounds the men as they convince the guard to seek asylum. His actions have put him on the top of the military's hit list, and several men chaperone him to the U.S. Embassy. The commotion attracts the attention of other G2s. Police cars creep past the church. Cecilia frowns at the smug look on one of the officer's face, as his hand hangs outside the window, pointing a gun and slamming it on the window ledge.

"That officer is going to shoot someone," Cecilia whispers to Maria.

A couple of seconds pass as the crowd waits, whispering and hoping the procession will soon begin. Suddenly, the guard's finger engages as he is pointing the gun. The sound of a gunshot sends the parishioners ducking for cover. Women in the crowd scream over a young man who lies on the ground, bleeding. Many in the group scatter, while several stay tending to the injured man. An ambulance rushes him to the hospital, and a group of parishioners, Cecilia, and Maria arrive a short time later.

"How is he doing?" Cecilia asks a man.

"We don't know," the man responds. "A friend called his mom. We're waiting for her to show up."

Several minutes pass when Cecilia looks at the door as a cane peaks through. A short, stocky woman controls the stick, stammering into the hospital. The whites of her eyes, replaced by a dull yellow, fill with teardrops. Other family members follow her. She presents herself at the registration desk, and the nurse leads her to the back of the room. The nurse disappears through a set of doors after asking the woman to wait.

In the lobby of the hospital, the crowd stares, waiting for an update. A couple of minutes pass when a doctor appears next to the woman. His lips move slowly and he solemnly places his hand on her shoulder. He pauses, and the woman faints. A family member catches her limp body, while others wail and scream.

Cecilia gasps and covers her mouth. She looks at Maria, noticing a tear roll down her cheek. The rest of the crowd sobs and hugs each other. A family member comes over and confirms their fears.

"The doctor said there was nothing they could do," the man says. "The bullet punctured a vital artery." A woman from the crowd embraces the young man's family member, as he is unable to hold back his grief.

A couple of days later, a group of parishioners go to pay their respects. They arrive at a barricade of G2s in front of the funeral home.

"This is unbelievable," Cecilia says in disbelief. "First they kill an innocent man, and now they keep us from giving our condolences!"

"Keep it down," Maria says. "The guards will take you away."

The crowd stands across the street, grieving in silence until the deceased is taken to the cemetery.

The following day, Samuel goes to a restaurant with Cecilia to plant another bomb. Cristian visits a bank to hide an explosive in an empty closet, while Pablo stops in a federal office building, doing the same. Other rebels place additional bombs throughout the city. The explosives use watches set to go off after everyone leaves the premises. Unlike Fidel's revolution against Batista, the rebels keep civilians safe, while disturbing Fidel's businesses. These are dangerous times and operations, but the rebels are not going to let Fidel take away their freedoms.

25 – The Binder

Cubans flee the island as the situation worsens.
America expands the embargo on Cuba. The Fidel regime
enforces more food rations. The government places
restrictions on how many pounds of meat, poultry, rice,
eggs, and coffee a person can purchase per month. To
survive and avoid hunger, Cubans find other means to
obtain food. The clandestine newspapers report updates of
people thrown in jail for days without a trial and thousands
shot by firing squad at the wall. Fidel shuts down radio
stations and newspapers and bans Christmas celebrations.

1962

1962 arrives with no end to the revolution in sight.
Since Samuel's incarceration, the brothers have been
unemployed. Papa helps them financially with the
impression that they are full-time students, fully committed
to their studies. Now, more than ever, the brothers
continue with their fight for democracy.

One morning, a group gathers in an empty
warehouse. A member stands guard outside as the brothers
run a training session.

In the corner, Cristian organizes weapons with another rebel. Recruits watch the men demonstrate how to clean and assemble guns. With caution, Cristian hands trainees loaded firearms.

To the side, Samuel and a couple of other rebels give instructions on firing a gun. Trainees get settled at their assigned stations for shooting practice. Samuel stands at the far end, assisting a couple of ladies. A Marilyn Monroe look-alike holds a weapon for the first time with a shaky hand. Samuel wraps his arms around her, directing her on the proper grip. His suave technique puts her at ease, and then he stays near her for additional guidance.

Other rebels walk behind the trainees, checking stance and aim. The gunshots and clicking of chambers, when reloaded, make Samuel's trainee anxious. She stands, holding the gun the way Samuel guided her. He gives her additional direction then steps to the side. With a slow and jittery finger, she pulls the trigger.

"Ricochet!" Samuel yells, collapsing. Frantic, she drops the weapon running to his side.

"Oh, my God! What have I done?" She cries.

"Got you," Samuel laughs.

"You jerk!" she scolds him.

The training ends in the early afternoon. Small groups of members disperse, to stay off G2s' radars. The brothers lock up the warehouse as Cristian turns around noticing a comrade approaching.

"I'm glad I caught you," the man says.

"Is everything ok?" Cristian asks.

"Bonifacio wanted me to give you this note," he replies handing Samuel a note.

Samuel reads the note to Cristian, "He needs to meet me urgently."

"Ok, be careful," Cristian, responds. "I'll see you tonight."

Samuel heads to the Paseo del Prado Park. *Why does the head of the National Student Group have to speak to me immediately,* he thinks to himself. *Is there a new movement? No, they would discuss that at their meeting tomorrow. Did he lose another friend to this regime?* His blood starts to boil, and he clenches his jaw. Samuel shakes his head. *I sound like Cristian, imagining the worse.*

When he arrives at the park, he casually strolls, scouting the grounds for guards or Fidel's spies. With the coast clear, he walks over to the lion monument when he spots Bonifacio on the concrete seat. He brushes lint off his suit, then tips his hat up, casually looking around, and then giving Samuel a smirk when he spots him. Underneath his hands and white knuckles, Bonifacio clutches a thick binder.

"Hi hermano," Samuel says.

Bonifacio stands up to hug Samuel. "Hello, brother."

"Good to see you again. What's going on?"

"Sit down," Bonifacio whispers. "They're chasing me. I need to leave right away."

"What happened?"

"It's safer if you don't know."

"You've got me worried. What can we do? Do you want Cristian to hide you? Do you need money?" The brothers never hesitate when rebels need help. They are thrifty with the funds Papa sends them, and Samuel is very generous, often giving money to those in need.

"No, I'm leaving the country. I'm running to the United States embassy, and asking for political asylum."

"Do you need me to contact someone for you?"

"I need you to take my place and take over. We need to win this revolution." He hands Samuel the binder. "Guard it with your life," he warns. "All our secret documents from the revolution are in here."

Samuel reaches for the binder. He pictures Papa working in the fincas again, Mama taking the grandchildren to their mango orchards, and Cristian waving to him at the university. He grasps the binder. "It's my honor brother. I'll guard it with my life. You can count on me."

"You're in charge now. Viva Cuba Libre, my brother!" He pats Samuel on the back and flees the park.

One week later, Francisco, the head of another rebel group, initiates a movement throughout all the provinces. Rebel police officers will provide weapons for the movement.

One evening, Cristian and Samuel walk down the busy downtown avenue. Cristian opens the door to the restaurant, discreetly scanning the crowd as Samuel walks in. At the back of the restaurant, all the heads of groups sit drinking colas. Francisco delegates jobs for each member and group, as he gives all members their pick-up locations and assignments.

"You two will retrieve some arsenal from a guard," Francisco instructs Samuel and Cristian.

"Ok, where do we meet him?" Samuel inquires.

"He will be waiting for you at this intersection," Francisco hands Samuel a paper with an address.

26 – Stairs

A few months into the New Year, Fidel officially takes control of the country. Fidel lets his spies loose on the island.

1962

A few days before the rebel attack, Fidel's military captures Francisco. In prison, he cracks during the tortures when they promise him clemency. The guards coerce the plan out of him. To protect himself, he gives up rebels' names and locations. Claiming Samuel leads the movement and possesses all the weapons. Fidel sends his army out to detain the rebels, with Samuel at the top of the list.

On August 30, 1962, Cristian prepares for the evening. He runs errands for his group when Pablo catches up to him.

"Cristian, we have to find Samuel. He can't go home!" Pablo warns him.

"Why, what's wrong?" Cristian asks.

"We've heard they're waiting for him."

"Who's waiting for him?"

"G2s!"

"Goddamit! Let's go!" They rush to the park where Samuel should be waiting.

Samuel walks to the furniture store where Maria works. He peaks in, knocking on the door window when he spots her at the counter. "How are you?" Maria salutes Samuel as she lets him in.

"Hi. Thanks for letting me in," Samuel responds.

"You look anxious."

"Tonight's it. We are taking down Fidel."

"Finally, we can have a democratic government. Life as it should be."

"What if something goes wrong?"

"Nothing's going to go wrong. Francisco has a good plan. Everything's in order. You'll see, it'll all work out. Com'on, where's the optimistic Samuel we know?"

"I know you're right. Alright, I have to go and get ready. See you tomorrow. It'll be a brand new day," Samuel hugs Maria before he leaves.

At the park, Cristian feels like he has lost his son in a crowd. He surveys the area. Dodging around people and looking around monuments.

"Over there," Pablo points. They rush to give Samuel the warning.

"I have to go home and get the binder," Samuel says.

"Forget the binder!" Cristian urges. "Let's just go to our station."

"I'll be fine. I'll be careful and fast."

The boys arrive outside Samuel's building.

Cristian once again pleads with him not to go in. "I have a bad feeling, brother!" Cristian knows of other times when Fidel's men surprise individuals as they walk into their homes.

"Don't worry; I'll be quick and careful. If I see or hear anything, I'll run out. Wait for me at the café."

"No! I don't like this. I'm waiting here."

"Captain's orders. Go to the café and wait," Samuel smirks at the men. "We have to make sure this plan goes through. I'll meet you there as planned."

Cristian and Pablo separate while Samuel goes up. Pablo stays close by keeping an eye on the building. Cristian takes small steps, turning around frequently. He turns the corner, and a heavy pit sits in his stomach. *I should turn around and go back*, he tells himself. *Samuel will be pissed, but I don't care. What if I'm overreacting? I do it all the time. Samuel's been down this road before. He knows what to do.* Cristian reassures himself.

Samuel walks into his guesthouse, giving the young lady at the desk a wink. She gives him a subtle sign to warn him, but he rushes in without noticing. He heads up the stairs, intently listening for any commotion. With soft footsteps, he walks down the hall to his room. Quickly, he puts the key in the lock, opens the door, and sees three G2s standing in his apartment. His heart drops. He realizes his fate.

"Get down on your knees and put your hands behind your head!" a G2 commands.

As they shove Samuel to his knees, Cristian's words flash through his mind. *Why didn't I listen to my brother?* Then he remembers tonight's rebellion. *The government will come down tonight, and I'll be free.* He tries to console himself.

The G2s shove him out the door, leading him down the stairs quickly and quietly. An unmarked government car waits in front of the building. Guards throw Samuel into the vehicle, and it speeds away.

Pablo is petrified when he sees the event. In disbelief, he flicks his cigarette on the ground, then rushes to the café. Skirting around pedestrians, he runs down the busy sidewalks, frantic to reach Cristian.

At the café, Cristian sits down while he waits. His restless leg and shaky hand catch the attention of a child. Time passes, the others do not show up, and panic sets. It has been too long! He turns around to notice Pablo running. Out of breath, he recounts the events to Cristian.

In despair, Cristian looks for the nearest phone. He calls the house, and the girls, at the reception desk, urge him to stay away; they are looking for him, too. Enraged, he slams the phone. A whirlwind of questions fill his mind. *What happened to his brother? What are they doing to Samuel? What is he going to do? The movement!* He thinks to himself. With a sense of hope, he regains his composure. "Let's go!" he says to Pablo. "We will take Fidel down tonight, and Samuel will be free."

"What are we waiting for? Let's go, brother!" Pablo responds.

At that moment, Fidel's army marches into police stations all over the island. They detain many officers. G2s stand guard in the stations waiting for the attack.

Cristian and Pablo head to the park, where others gather for final preparations on the assault. Before midnight, Cristian and Pablo make their way to the police station. The men scout the corner to keep an eye out for their police contact. A cat catches Cristian's attention, and an eerie silence on the streets alarms them.

Midnight strikes. Their guard contact is nowhere in sight. The men hide out at a local park, awake all night. Cristian paces back and forth, kicking trees. Pablo tries to calm him down. At daylight, they meet at a park with other comrades, who inform them of the night's events.

"The G2s ambushed the police stations," one rebel says.

"They captured many rebels," another one responds. "Other rebels have gone into hiding or sought asylum at the embassy."

"With Samuel in jail, they will come after you next, Cristian," another man announces. "You should leave."

"I'm not going anywhere! I have to find Samuel and get him out of there!" Cristian shouts.

"Alright, brother. We understand. At least take cover somewhere," Pablo pats him on the back. "We'll find him."

Cristian seeks shelter at a friend's house.

27 – Metal Room

1962

Days pass after Samuel's capture, and Cristian wanders like a nomad. He can't stay in one place too long, or he will jeopardize getting caught or putting others in danger. Cristian makes the agonizing call home. He informs Alejandro, the only family member aware of their involvement with the revolution, of the turn of events.

"What can we do?" he pleads with Alejandro.

"We will get our attorney to the Havana courthouse right away!" Alejandro reassures him.

"Ok, I'll keep checking in with you," Cristian responds. "If you need to reach me, the girls at the house know how to find me."

Cristian tries to be optimistic. Samuel was captured for several days last time and eventually let go. It tears him up inside, thinking of what his little brother will suffer. He remembers what Samuel endured last time.

At La Cabaña prison, guards continuously drag Samuel from a bright room to a pitch-black room, to disorient him. They throw him in a room so hot and humid the walls drip with moisture, but he reveals nothing.

"I'm a student at the University of Havana," Samuel scoffs, with as much energy as he can manage.

"You are the leader of this movement!" the guard gets in his face, spitting as he talks.

"No, I'm not! I don't know what the hell you're talking about. I'm just a student."

The guards lock him in a cold metal room, depriving him of food and water. Hours pass as his body quivers uncontrollably. His teeth chatter as he huddles in the corner. Thoughts race through his head. *What will happen? Will he survive the tortures this time? Did the rebels succeed? Is Cristian injured?* His extremities feel numb. He must focus on warm thoughts to survive. *Imias,* he thinks to himself. *The sun baking the hills, the breeze warm on his cheeks as he walks along the beach.* A crack on the door snaps him out of his thoughts. The door opens to expose a bright light that blinds him. Guards yank him out, dragging him back to the interrogation room.

"What's your next plan? We know you're in charge!"

"I'm a student!" he tries to persuade them. "You're the government, check the records!"

"We have proof that you are leading the coup!" the guard yells.

Samuel knows they are bluffing. The only job he had was to pick up some weapons.

The guards return Samuel to his cell, "I need to contact my family," Samuel calls out.

"You will do nothing but sit here and rot, you traitor," the guard scowls.

Samuel sits, leaning against the hard concrete wall, lost in his thoughts as he gazes out the barred window. Looking up at the twinkling lights in the sky, he reminisces on the clear nights back home. He longs for the talks and laughs he shared with Cristian on their long walks to the pastures. He would do anything to be back in Imias right now.

In Havana, the family's lawyer alerts Alejandro that Samuel will receive a military trial. "A trial for treason is what Samuel will be facing."

"What are his chances for a release?" Alejandro asks.

"Not good," the lawyer alerts Alejandro. "Fidel's reputation with these trials is to impose severe consequences."

"What does that mean?"

"I will plead for jail time to spare his life."

The attorney gives Alejandro the day and time for Samuel's visitations. He rushes to La Cabaña in Havana to see him, but does not succeed.

"Family visitation times for this prisoner was earlier in the day," a guard informs him.

"This is the time our family was given," he says.

"You missed your visitation time," the guard repeats.

Crumpling up the paper in his hand, Alejandro insists, "I demand to see whoever is in charge! I want to see my brother!"

"You can't see him. Don't worry. Your brother is fine," a general states. "You can see him at his court date."

He worries about his little brother, and wonders if *all the stories he's heard about Fidel's prisoners are true?* In disbelief that this is happening to his family, a disheartened Alejandro, contacts Cristian.

"Samuel's court date is September 20th," Alejandro's voice cracks as he tells Cristian. "They wouldn't let me see him."

"Those bastards!" Cristian punches the wall. His hand burns, but he is numb to the pain.

"Don't go anywhere. I'll keep you posted that day."

"Ok, brother," Cristian clears his throat as he says goodbye.

28 – The Gavel

1962

On September 20, 1962, Samuel lies in a cell with several other political prisoners, some whom he knows. Guards call Samuel and 15 others out of their cell that morning. In silence, they make the walk as guards shove them. They step into a room, and are ordered to sit on the ground until a guard calls them. Several minutes pass when a G2 summons Samuel and leads him into another room.

A general sits at a desk, staring at a book with names.

"Samuel Enriquez," the general announces.

"Yes," Samuel responds.

"Samuel Enriquez you are charged with treason. You can plead your case at a military trial. Get him out of here!" the general announces.

Samuel holds his head up as he walks back to the holding room. After all the men receive their charges, guards usher them back to their cell. Samuel solemnly walks in, taking a seat by a friend.

"I'm going down," Samuel mumbles.

"Don't say that. Your family has a good attorney. He'll get you a lesser sentence," his friend reassures him. "Don't give up my friend. You have always been a rock and the strongest of all."

Samuel knows their attorney is both good at his job and a good friend of the family. Most of Papa's business associates became good friends of the family. Money was not a problem. Samuel knows Papa has plenty of money put away. *What if Fidel took it all? The government has done it to other families. What if Papa spends all his hard-earned money keeping him from the firing squad?* He is flooded with guilt. *Mama is probably having a nervous breakdown, and Papa must be furious. He will give up his dream of living in the city and help Papa with the business when he gets out. What if he doesn't get out?*

At 2 p.m., a crowd gathers outside the courtroom. Samuel's supporters wait for the door to open.

A court attendant steps out into the hallway. "The trial has been suspended," she announces.

"What! That's unacceptable!" a man shouts.

"You can't do that!" a woman screams in protest.

"What is the meaning of this?" Cecilia demands. "Why is it suspended? What are they doing?"

The crowd protests and demands answers, causing the worried attendant to retreat into the courtroom. The group gets louder as men pace and women's eyes fill with tears. Everyone worries about Samuel's fate.

"Ok everyone, settle down. We'll stay and wait for an update," a couple of ladies announce. "We'll get the word out as soon as we hear something."

Several minutes pass as the crowd dwindles. Suddenly, the courtroom doors open, and the ladies rush in. The judge sits at his bench as several defendants sit at their table. Attorneys assemble next to some of the accused. Guards stand by the exits as a prosecuting attorney speaks to the court.

"They lied! The trial is going on as scheduled," one lady announces. "Go let the others know."

As the trial goes on, supporters fill the public gallery in a mannerly fashion as the judge pounds the gavel. "All members of the public attending will sit silently or be sentenced for public disturbance," the judge announces.

Fifteen political prisoners sit accused in the courtroom. The men and women sit motionless, awaiting their fate. One by one, their attorneys plead their cases. Samuel and two others are on trial for the government's most severe accusations. Their trials will be last. Staying out of jail is not in the cards for these men. The lawyers focus on keeping them alive.

In the defense box, Samuel's attorney leans in, "Plead guilty," he advises Samuel.

"No!" Samuel responds. "I didn't do what they're accusing me of."

"It will save your life. Plead guilty."

"If I plead guilty, I have to turn in my brother and friends. I know why I'm here. That coward accused me to save his skin. I will not send anyone to the lion's den."

"Samuel, I implore you! Please plead guilty!"

"I didn't do any of those things. I'm sorry, but NO!"

"Samuel Enriquez, how do you plead?" the judge asks.

Samuel stands up. Puts his hand on his attorney's shoulder, "I am an innocent student who just wants to finish his studies," he says.

His two comrades follow suit. Outraged by their insubordination, the judge passes a sentence. "Samuel Enriquez, on the charges of leading the rebellion against the government, supplying weapons, and refusing to confess, you are hereby sentenced to death!" The judge strikes the gavel and the crowd gasps.

Samuel's face goes pale. His attorney drops his head, as the two other rebels close their eyes. Silent sobs echo in the courtroom as tears stream down faces of those who just heard the verdict. Friends embrace each other for consolation. Everyone restrains comments and outbursts, afraid of the government's retaliation.

Shock consumes the three men. Crushed and defeated, they sit in utter silence with their heads down, holding back tears and in fear of their future. The gleam in Samuel's eyes fades away. His life begins to flash before his eyes as he digests the severity of his sentence. Devastated, the three men condemned to death stagger out of the courtroom. The other rebels sentenced to jail follow. They are beaten and brokenhearted.

Samuel's attorney approaches the judge's bench to begin the appeal. The lawyer pleads, displaying a thick stack of documents, proving Samuel's good character, straight A grades from the university, clean police record, and documents showing the Enriquez business certificates. With a slam of the gavel, the judge argues the proof of traitorous acts. The attorney asks for the documents with the evidence, but the judge denies his request.

29 – The Wall

1962

Late that afternoon, Cristian anxiously waits for news at a friend's house.

"I'm sure they'll call soon," his friend tells him.

Cristian paces back and forth, "I'm so worried about him. I don't think he'll be as lucky as last time."

"Think positive, my friend."

The phone rings. Cristian stops mid-step, feeling queasy.

"It's for you," his friend announces.

Cristian walks over to the table as his friend hands him the phone. Leaning against the wall, Cristian grabs the phone.

"How are you doing?" Alejandro asks.

"I'm all right," Cristian responds. "What happened?"

"It's not good."

"What happened?" The line is silent. "What happened?" Cristian yells.

"He will be put to death. Tomorrow."

Cristian's knees buckle and he drops to the ground. He feels the urge to cry out but is paralyzed in disbelief. He bangs the back of his head on the wall, gasping for air. In agony and at a loss for words, the brothers decide to meet at the park.

At the park, Cristian sits on a bench scouting his surroundings. Alejandro runs over when he spots Cristian.

He gives Cristian a big hug and whispers, "Happy Birthday brother." The importance of the day had slipped Cristian's mind. They should be celebrating today, instead of grieving. "I spoke with Papa." Alejandro informs him. "He wanted me to tell you to not feel guilty. It's not your fault!"

"We were together! How could I not feel guilty?" Cristian hollers. "We're always together, same university, same degree, and the same cause. I'm his older brother. I'm supposed to watch over him! I told him I would have his back. Goddamit, I told him not to go. I should have stopped him!"

"Let's pray for our brother."

"Pray? Pray to who? There's no one watching over us!"

"Don't say that Cristian."

"No, there is no God! A God would not let this happen. No! I'm not praying."

"Come on, Cristian." Alejandro pats Cristian's shoulder. Unable to control his pain any more, Cristian begins to sob and shake uncontrollably. Alejandro embraces him while they stand in the park, weeping silently.

Cristian spends the rest of the night on a park bench. His hands cover his eyes as he agonizes over the turn of events and the fate of his brother. How he wishes he could see him one more time, as he wipes the tears streaming down his face. He relives that fateful day over and over again. *If only he could turn back time.*

Earlier that day, guards had transported Samuel to a gallery at La Cabaña. The regime ensures he does not see his cellmates again. Eight other men wait in the room as Samuel walks in. Several men kneel praying on the cold concrete floor. Others lie in front of the barred window, hoping heaven hears their pleas. Three look up to see who joined them. They make eye contact and give him a nod. Samuel kneels by the window, clasping his hands together to rests his head on top of them. His mind floods with thoughts of his family. *How will this affect his parents? Why did he ignore Cristian's advice? He will not see his nieces and nephews grow up. He did not get a chance to tell his girlfriend he loves her.* A tear rolls down his face when a commotion grabs his attention. Samuel wipes his face then turns around.

Guards walk in, demanding that everyone line up. The men get up, crying their final prayers. Guards shove, push, and pull the political prisoners who take their time. Samuel, being one of them, yanks his arm away from the guard giving the guard a defiant look. The guard points his gun.

Samuel yells, "Go ahead!"

Another political prisoner yells, "Samuel, don't antagonize him!"

Samuel responds, "Why not? He's going to kill me either way!"

The guard puts down his gun then orders Samuel to move. Knowing his fate, he concedes and starts to walk, but he will go with pride and without being bullied. These Communists will not intimidate him.

On September 21st, at 1:28 a.m., the nine men trudge in the hallway, towards the courtyard. A female guard stands watch at the entrance to the yard. She reminds Samuel of someone. *How he wishes he could see her again.*

As he arrives at the patio entry, he murmurs to her, "Take me in your heart because they are killing mine tonight!"

Cold stone cells with barred windows surround the open space. The men are numb to the giant raindrops that pierce their skin in the downpour. Guards continue to shove the men as they solemnly walk, stepping in puddles of water along the way. They come to a halt when they reach the wall.

"Face the wall!" a guard demands.

Men cry for mercy and prayers get louder as the firing squad marches away behind them. Guards line up, aim, and the general sounds off.

Samuel shouts, "Viva Cuba Libre!" His words echo through the courtyard into cells. Men inside chant Viva Cuba Libre, Viva Cristo Rey, Live Christ the King.

A shower of gunshots echoes through the courtyard as nine bodies drop to the ground. The rain continues to pound on their bodies. The clear puddles run red with bloodshed. Samuel struggles to take his final breath, thinking only of his family, of his brother. He is too weak to even pray. His ragged breaths stops and he lays lifeless. All of his hopes, dreams, and ambitions were violently stolen at the hands of a brutal, murderous dictator.

"Killers! Cowards!" prisoners yell from their cells.

At 4 a.m., that morning, the attorney sits in the courtroom appealing Samuel's case as a guard brings the judge a note.

"It's done," the judge informs the lawyer. He drops to his knees. *What an injustice*, he thinks to himself. *Samuel never stood a chance.*

30 – New Head

1962

The girls from the guesthouse contact Maria early in the morning. They inform Maria that guards will bury Samuel soon. She picks up Cecilia, and they rush to the cemetery. In utter shock, they sob uncontrollably during the longest walk of their lives. They are grief stricken and the walk feels like an eternity. When they arrive at the cemetery, they spot the drab olive green military pickup truck. It contains the coffins. They stand to the side, watching and waiting.

A guard spots the women. "Turn around! Go wait off the grounds!" he scolds them. "Do not come back until we are done burying the bodies!"

They curse underneath their breath and stomp away. "Oh my God, why is this happening?" Maria cries out.

"There's no God!" Cecilia screams in agony.

"Why, God? Why?"

"God does not exist."

"If he did, this wouldn't have happened." The women huddle together in anguish, trembling as they weep. As the truck begins to pull out, the women rush over, demanding to know the location of Samuel's gravesite. One of the guards checks his log then gives the women the number to the site.

They walk to Samuel's final resting place, crying and protesting. At the gravesite, they drop to the ground. Their knees sink in the mud while they scream and gasp for air. Streams of tears fall on the fresh soil. At the edge of the gravel path, a petite rebel with short blonde hair walks towards them. Samuel's clandestine girlfriend appears with bloodshot eyes. Samuel was a hopeless romantic, always enchanting ladies, but romance is dangerous in a revolution. Many rebels stay away from relationships or have them in secrecy to protect one another. The government refuses to allow a formal funeral.

In Imias, the attorney informs Papa that the government denied their request for a family burial. Heartbroken, Papa weeps in disbelief that he has lost his 26-year-old son. He hides in the store that he now works in, instead of owning, mourning the loss of his youngest. Praying and gasping for air as he chokes on his tears, he cannot conceive of how vicious a human being can be. His son was not taken by illness, accident, or a force of nature, but by assassination from a ruthless tyrant. This heartless Communist did not even allow the family to say goodbye.

A couple of weeks later, groups gather in secrecy at a supporter's house. Cubans are enraged at the turn of events and the crimes committed by this Communist Dictator. The assembly nominates Cristian as the new leader of the student group. He grieves in ways no one can imagine, but the fury flowing through his veins fuels his thirst for revenge.

After the meeting, Cristian steps out into the street. He thinks back to a conversation he had with Samuel. Before the last movement, the brothers made a pact to leave the country if it failed. "Sorry brother. I have to break our pact," Cristian talks to the heavens.

Pablo joins Cristian outside, "We have lost many good people," Cristian tells him.

"Don't worry," Pablo reassures him. "We'll grow strong again."

"I will get Fidel for what he's done!" he proclaims.

"We're here to help you. Lead the way!"

A week later, rebels begin their quest to recruit others and reignite the movement. Their numbers are drastically down, making it difficult to find new comrades. Cristian meets several times with Pablo and the militant heads of other student groups. The rebels meet at different restaurants to discuss new strategies.

Several days have passed when groups assemble at the Park Antonio Mateo, a favorite hangout. With this large gathering, the rebels spread out to appear like a casual get-together. Cristian mingles with a group of university students by the monument. Cecilia chats on a bench with a group of business students. She carries a message for him, and he cannot wait to see her again. Thinking about her gives him a glimpse of hope and much-needed joy.

After a few minutes, Cristian pats a friend on the shoulder then casually walks over to Cecilia. He sits next to her, and their knees accidentally touch. She quickly moves her leg away. *Wow, she really must not like me,* Cristian thinks!

"Hi, Cecilia. Good to see you again," Cristian says.

"How are you?" she responds. "I'm so sorry about your loss. So many of us were shocked and deeply distraught by Samuel's assassination," she said in a kind and gentle tone. Her voice was soothing.

"Thank you!" Cristian's voice cracks as he holds back his tears.

"He was an amazing man and a true patriot. He will be deeply missed." She hugs him. Her hands offer a feeling of comfort and warmth.

Cristian puts an arm around her, feeling safe and a sense of peace. He aches to bury his head in her shoulder, release all his anger and sorrow, but he forces himself to keep it bottled up.

"Oh, your message," she says, ending the embrace to dig in her purse. "Here you go."

"Thank you," Cristian responds.

"Let me know what you need. I want to get this Communist criminal out of here!"

"I'll be in touch soon."

Slowly the groups disperse to avoid drawing suspicion.

31 – The Boat

Months pass with fear running rampant on the island. The severe consequences for opposing Fidel makes it very hard to recruit rebels. Cristian heads home from work to meet Pablo and discuss ways to attract more warriors. At the café, they sit down and start brainstorming some ideas. A rebel spy, who infiltrated the military, spots them and sprints over.

"Don't go home!" she warns him.

"Why, what's wrong?" Cristian asks.

"They are waiting for you. The guards went through all your things and are sitting at your apartment waiting."

"You're not going home!" Pablo orders. "You better not be as stubborn as your brother."

"I won't, I promise." Cristian heeds her warning and finds shelter with a family who harbors rebels in hiding. At dinnertime, they sit to watch the news, when a government broadcast interrupts the show.

Fidel captures group leaders and uses them as pawns on live TV. Fidel threatens to harm the prisoners' families if they do not comply. The degraded men are forced to demand that all rebels terminate the battle. The prisoners state that group leaders who do not obey will put their families in danger. They warn that government spies have penetrated all the groups.

Cristian fears for his family. He feels responsible for his brother's assassination, despite the consolations from his family that he is not at fault. He needs to take drastic measures to protect the rest of the family.

Pablo accompanies Cristian to a beach in Oriente with a group fleeing the country. When they reach the shore, the large gathering overwhelms them. Laughter and singing fill the atmosphere as people celebrate their departure, confident they will escape tonight. Doctors, factory workers, families, young, old, and pregnant women rejoice as the boat gets near.

The boat that will take them to Puerto Rico floats on the horizon. To ensure they make it on board, people stampede into the water. It drifts in as close as possible to shore. Boarding begins on the vessel, and it quickly gets dangerously crowded. The hull gets deeper and deeper in the water as people continue to board. People start to panic.

"The boat is sinking!" a woman yells.

"There're too many people," a man screams. "No one else can get on!"

A dad lifts his son to his wife on the boat. On the side of the vessel, a woman pleads for help as she tries to climb on. No one helps.

"We're overcrowded," the captain makes a plea. "If you're not in danger or being chased by the government, please get off the ship."

No one listens, and the boat continues sinking.

"We're here to take those seeking asylum or in danger from Fidel," he repeats.

Cristian falls in that category and needs to be on this boat, but no one complies. He makes the sacrifice, jumping off the ship along with Pablo and several others.

As Cristian heads back to shore, he sees people pointing out to the sea. A man flounders drowning, apparently after falling off the boat. Without hesitation, Cristian jumps in and swims out. He reaches the man, who can barely keep his head above water. Cristian wraps his arms around him, making sure the man's nose and mouth are above water, he swims back to shore. The men crawl to safety on the sand away from the tide. Cristian drops from exhaustion. The man slowly comes to, and then staggers away.

Cristian, completely exhausted, dozes off. Several hours later, he wakes up startled to be under a canopy of sea grapes. Groggy, he tries to recall the day's event. *How long was he out?* He wonders.

"I dragged you off to the side when I saw you collapse," Pablo whispers.

Startled by his voice, Cristian responds, "Thank you, brother, for sticking by me!"

"You're fortunate a guard didn't spot you lying on the beach. Someone must be watching over you."

Cristian looks to the heavens. "I think Samuel is sending me a message."

"Fidel is still looking for you. We have to lay low until the groups figure out a plan."

The men find refuge at another hideout. "Come in," the lady of the house greets them.

On the verge of passing out, Cristian leans on Pablo. "Help me with him!" Pablo begs.

"What happened to him?" the man of the house asks.

"He collapsed after rescuing a man from the water," Pablo explains. "He hasn't been feeling well since."

"He's burning up," the lady notices after putting her hand on his head. "Lay him on the sofa. I'll take his temperature."

The ordeal leaves Cristian sick with a fever. His friends get him a doctor, and they stay put for a week while he recuperates. After his recovery, they return to Havana.

Several months pass. The rest of the Enriquez family now stays in Santiago. Papa answers the door to let in the family doctor, and they stand at the door quietly discussing the plan.

"How is she today?" the doctor asks.

"Today is a little better," Papa responds. "We need to give her the horrible news of Samuel's murder. We can't put it off any longer."

"I have the sedatives. It will help Mama cope with the devastating news."

"Is it safe, doctor?" Alejandro asks.

"Very safe. I'll stay a while. Having the family around her will help."

Papa leads the doctor to their bedroom. "Good afternoon, Señora," the doctor greets Mama.

"Hello, doctor," Mama responds in a soft, weak voice.

"Doctor has a new treatment for you," Papa says.

"Okay," she complies, sitting calmly while the doctor administers the sedative. The family gathers in the bedroom.

Several minutes pass when Papa gently holds his wife's hand, "We have distressing news, Mama," Papa mumbles with a heavy heart. "Samuel has been murdered by Fidel's guards."

"What?" Mama responds.

"Mama, Samuel was captured by Fidel's men and assassinated," Alejandro speaks slowly.

"No! Samuel is at school with Cristian."

"He was, Mama, but now he is gone," Papa adds.

"No! I don't believe you. I need to see him."

"You can't, Mama, Samuel is gone," Alejandro restates.

"No, no, no. I don't believe you."

"I'm sorry, Mama, but it's true."

"Nooo! Not my baby. Why? Why my baby?"

Mama sobs uncontrollably as the family unsuccessfully tries to console her. The doctor administers additional medication to calm her down. For the next few days, the doctor makes daily visits to monitor her and provide additional sedatives, while Papa sits by her side.

As the days go on, she weeps and cries out, "Why would someone do something so horrible? How could a human being be so monstrous?"

Papa continues to comfort Mama as she mourns; imagining the nightmare her son had to endure. Papa tries to ease her pain, but struggles himself as he thinks back to the words that Fidel spoke when he overthrew Batista.

"I want to tell the people and the mothers of Cuba that I will resolve all the problems without spilling a drop of blood. I tell mothers that never, because of us, will they have to cry." He has done nothing but lie to Cubans from the very beginning. Papa weeps.

Fidel claims his hands are clean of blood because, in Cuba, they only shoot assassins or terrorists. *More lies,* Papa thinks to himself; *Samuel was neither of those.* The family now lives on constant watch of their once tenacious Mama.

32 – An Offer

1963

On April 5, 1963, Cristian heads to meet friends for a bite at the bar La Pampa. He sees two men in suits, standing in front of the bar, staring at him. Their intense stare makes Cristian suspicious, forcing him to cross the street. Casually, he keeps walking, stepping into a grocery store, when a pay phone grabs his attention, and he decides to check in with a friend. She cautions him to be careful because G2s captured many rebels this afternoon. He gets a bad vibe and peeks outside. With no suspicious characters in sight, he decides to head to his destination to hash out a plan with the group. He wonders if his friends are waiting at La Pampa or if G2s captured them? Suddenly an object shoved into his back brings him to a halt.

"You are under arrest!" a guard says. "Get in the car!"

His heart drops to the pit of his stomach as a car pulls up. *This is surreal*, Cristian thinks to himself, as his mind races during the longest ride of his life with thoughts of the peaceful days in Imias, wishing he could be with his little brother and return to the pastures. The stories Samuel told him of his time in prison play in his mind.

At the prison, they put him in a cell by himself. He sits in the stuffy concrete room for hours, sweating and staring up at the barred window, until guards arrive dragging him out. In the interrogation room with his hands tied, guards punch and kick him into the wall. Rage consumes him, and he kicks back. They tackle Cristian to the ground, with one holding him down, while the other continuously punches him. Unable to think of any other way to protect himself, Cristian tucks his head to block the blows. Furious that Cristian does not crack, the G2s yank him out of the room, taking him to the metal cell.

"Take off your clothes!" a G2 commands.

"Hell, no!" Cristian responds, and the beatings continue. Cristian drops to the ground, weak and injured. The guards jerk and tear the clothes off him then kick him into the cell.

Cristian spends hours in the unbearable cold. His body throbs from the welts and bruises from the beatings, with the pain getting stronger as his body quivers. Guards return, throwing a yellow prison uniform in the cell. Cristian slides the pants on, one leg at a time, groaning silently in his head to hide his pain from the guards. The fabric touching his skin repulses him, and reality sinks in that he will not go home when the guards push him down the corridor to his cell.

Weeks later, Cristian gets his day in court. His lawyer warns him of a 20-year sentence unless he pleads guilty and denounce his rebel group. Cristian refuses to cooperate. He receives a counteroffer: do not renounce, but plead guilty. Once again, he rejects the offer, and the judge condemns him to 12 years.

The family lawyer returns to Santiago to meet with Papa. "I tried, but Cristian would not budge," he tells Papa.

"I know, my friend," Papa responds. "Thank you for trying. We raised our sons to be tough and honorable men. They fought for their land and family and will always protect their family and friends." Papa is proud, but still filled with sorrow.

"I wish I could have done more."

"You've done all you can. I just need to digest all the turn of events," Papa's voice cracks. "First, my youngest son is murdered. Now, I find out Cristian will be incarcerated for 12 years. I don't know what this news is going to do to Mama. If only Samuel could have gotten the same sentence. I don't want either of them in jail, but at least he would be alive."

"I'm sorry. It makes no sense. Why Samuel's sentence was death, and Cristian's was imprisonment? They were both accused of treason."

"Nothing this villain does makes sense!" Papa insists.

"Did you tell Mama about Alberto?" the attorney asks.

"That he spent five months in prison?"

"Yes."

"No, I just told her he was working in Imias. I was ready to tell her until you informed me that you were able to prove him innocent of those outrageous government accusations."

"I still don't know why they think he was involved in illegal sales. And then, Alejandro. Detained with no explanation."

"I'm just glad they set him free." Papa pauses, slamming his fists on the table. "This vicious tyrant has taken over our island, stolen our property, assassinated my youngest child, and seems to be trying to take the rest, one by one. Is this a personal vendetta, or is he just the devil in disguise?"

"I don't know who or what he is, but he is evil."

"Thank you for all your help, my friend. Now, I have to break this news to Mama. I'm worried about what it will do to her health."

"Let me know if you need anything."

A week after Cristian's trial, the government moves him to Isla de Pinos, a prison on an island south of Havana. He shares his cell with another rebel. The men wear yellow uniforms to distinguish political prisoners from regular inmates.

A year passes. In the afternoon, guards usher Cristian and his friends to the dining hall. He sits at a wooden table in the dingy room anxiously waiting for his first two-hour yearly visit. The anxiety turns to hope as he witnesses others reuniting with loved ones until a guard walks up with a telegram.

> *Sorry mijo, we just received the telegram with your visitation time. We don't have enough time to make the trip. We will make arrangements to be there next time.*
>
> *Love, Papa*

A common tactic by the Communist party was to give less than 24 hours' notice.

At the table, he sits, head down, heartbroken, and dying to see his family. Desperately needing to see a smiling face and get a loving embrace, his eyes get glossy and feel heavy. He is losing hope. He blinks several times to clear the tears building up when he spots Cecilia. She visits another friend, and he decides to head over.

"Cristian, join us," his friend rejoices.

"Thank you, brother," Cristian responds.

"Hi, Cristian!" she stands up to embrace him, giving him the hug he needed.

"It's good to see you again," Cristian responds with a smile. The three spend their time catching up, cautious on the topics they discuss, determined not to compromise Cecilia.

That evening, Cristian lies in his bunk bed, in anguish over the turn of events. *All their hard work. Is there any hope? Is someone else strong enough to overturn this killer? Will they prevail? Is there a way out of the tortures, this unbearable and oppressive prison?* Thinking of Cecilia, and the next time she will visit, helps keep his hopes alive.

33 – Visits

1965

Another year goes by when Papa receives a telegram from the director of the prison. Once again, the government only gives them 24 hours for their scheduled visitation with Cristian. They have very little time to gather the items for Cristian's bag. Victor contacts Cecilia to let her know that he and Papa will be going to see Cristian. She joins them to give him additional support and updates.

Cecilia arrives early, walking past the compound of cylindrical buildings, agonizing that on the other side of those colossal buildings and cold walls are comrades who fought alongside her to take down a tyrant. *What can she do to help them*, she wonders? She steps in front of the stairs to the main building, a three-story, tan structure, waiting for Papa and Victor.

A short time later, Papa and Victor arrive. "Hi, Cecilia," Victor greets her.

"What did you bring him?" she asks, curious about the bag Papa carries.

"It was hard to pick with the 25 lb. allowance and rations," Victor responds. "We threw in as much of his favorites as we could: powdered milk, chocolate, grains, and crackers."

In the lobby, they wait for a guard to call the names of the prisoners waiting for visitors. They get in line when the G2 calls Cristian's name, and Cecilia notices a slender woman holding a bag, walking to the information desk.

"You did not call my son's name," she tells the guard.

"Then your son is not scheduled for visitors," the guard responds.

"Yes, he is. Here is the telegram from the government." She hands the guard the yellow paper.

He yanks it from her hands, grunting, then scans the letter and checks it against his list. "Oh, he was assassinated last night."

"Whaa." She passes out, and Cecilia rushes to her side.

"How," Cecilia begins to speak as Victor runs over to stop her.

"Don't say anything," Victor whispers. "You'll get in trouble."

"Did you hear how heartless he was?" Cecilia responds.

"I know and agree, but you know what they'll do to you if you talk back."

"What's going on!" Another guard steps in front of Victor.

"Nothing," Victor responds.

"We are just helping her," Cecilia says with a clenched fist on the ground.

"We'll take care of her. Leave her!" The guard barks as another G2 takes the woman and drags her away.

Cecilia wipes a tear from her face as Victor leads her to the line. A guard, with a thick beard in an army green uniform, stands with a paper and pen, writing their relationship to Cristian. She introduces herself as Cristian's wife; guards will not let her in otherwise. G2s direct the men and women to different rooms. Cecilia removes her clothes for the strip search.

"Hold your nose and jump," the female guard asks as she twirls her ponytail.

Cecilia follows the orders, fuming inside at the smirk on the guard's face. She knows if she does not comply, they can kick her out or make this place her new residence.

"Now cough," the guard demands, expecting something to fall out like the previous visitor she searched.

Guards expose the men to the same body search. When they are cleared and dressed, a balding guard hands back the bag they brought for Cristian.

"What's in here?" the guard asks.

"Powdered milk, chocolate, crackers, and a check," Papa responds as the guard pokes the bag with a knife to check the contents.

"Move on." The guard clears them, and they meet Cecilia in the corridor.

Military men lead the three to the dining hall. White, stale walls surround families conversing with prisoners at concrete tables and benches. A guard directs them to an empty table, and they anxiously sit chatting while they wait for Cristian to come out.

A few minutes later, Cristian walks into the dining hall, spotting his family. Papa gives him a long tearful embrace. Cristian tries to hold back the tears, but a few trickle down. Cecilia and Victor follow suit, overwhelming Cristian with joy at finally seeing loved ones. He smells a whiff of coffee on Victor, and memories of their finca flood his brain. *What can I do to get out of this wretched place?* He thinks to himself.

"How are they treating you?" Papa asks.

"As well as you can expect," he responds. "I'm surrounded by many friends, and we help each other stay strong." To spare them from worries, Cristian does not want to give his family too many details.

"Are you getting the monthly checks I send you?"

"Yes, thank you! I've been able to purchase some items."

In the cafeteria, they catch up. Despite Cristian's dire situation, he seems to be holding it together.

When their two hours are up, the farewells are emotionally draining. They know they probably will not see each other again for another year. The three stand, weeping as they watch a guard escort Cristian away.

Later that afternoon a guard hollers in the corridor, "Let's go! Line up!" The men line up. "Move it!" he continues to command.

In small groups, guards lead them to an empty room. "You know the drill, take it off," another guard demands. Guards shove them in a chamber like sardines, naked, poking them with sticks to cause the men to rub against each other, as they perform another unannounced strip search.

The guards laugh as they degrade the prisoners.

Back in his cell, Cristian recalls the hopeful events of his day. The support of his family helps him stay strong. Seeing Cecilia's bright green eyes fills him with hope.

34 - The Horizon

1968

A few years later, another short notice telegram arrives. This time only one family member may visit, forcing Papa to go by himself. Cristian's recent letters have been vague, concerning Papa, that Cristian might be keeping secrets and enduring the unspeakable acts many Cuban prisoners report. He decides to pry the truth out of his son.

Papa finally arrives after a long trip and checks in at the desk. "I'm here to see Cristian Enriquez," Papa announces.

"Visits are canceled today," the guard reports.

"I have this telegram," Papa hands it to the guard. "Today is my day to visit."

"No visits today!" the guard barks.

"I have come a long way!" Papa fumes. "Why am I not allowed to see my son?"

"All visits are canceled!" The guard begins to lose his patience.

Enraged, but afraid of retaliation from the government, Papa leaves with his bag of supplies he had packed for Cristian. He walks out slowly, hoping the guard will change his mind.

Papa's eyes fill with tears as he walks down the gravel road, unaware of the prison truck that just pulled out. Cristian sits in the bed of the truck with 40 other inmates. He looks on the road, towards the entrance, spotting a familiar figure. His eyes tear up, and his head drops when he realizes the man is his father. Why is he here? He worries.

Cristian infers that it was a visiting day. What a brutal tyrant to torture innocent family members. He wants to jump out of the truck or at least call out to him, but he must sit quietly, watching his father disappear into the horizon. Any dialogue falls under insubordination, resulting in severe consequences.

Months pass before Papa receives notice that the government has relocated Cristian to La Cabaña, a prison known for severe torture and hundreds of executions. He feels nauseous and disheartened, picturing Cristian in the most dismal place in Cuba.

At La Cabaña, Cristian walks into a concrete room filled with bunk beds, not nearly enough for the 500 prisoners with whom he shares the room. Men take turns sleeping on the thin canvas mattress bunk beds. The large gallery houses one bathroom for all to share. Unable to take daily showers, they save their drinking water for washing up.

Months later, the family receives the visitation date at the new prison. The short notice does not allow enough time to make the trip. Papa asks a female friend who lives nearby to go for the family and deliver messages.

She arrives at the penitentiary, an old Spanish fort. Guards lead visitors through the outdoor courtyard, sheltered by a tall saltwater stained brick wall. Family and friends walk by a wall with bullet holes and bloodstains, while gunmen describe the assassinations.

Inside the building, they take her to a room where a wire mesh separates inmates and visitors. Cristian walks in, startled to see a short, stocky woman, a longtime friend of the family.

"It's good to see you. Is everything ok at home? Has something happened?" Cristian asks.

She stares at the disheveled figure in front of her. "Everyone is fine. Your family had less than 24 hours' notice. Your dad knew he couldn't get here in time and asked me to come since I'm closer."

"That makes sense. I was worried for a second."

"Your dad wanted me to give you these messages."
She slips the notes through the holes in the fence, and they
take some time to catch up. She arrives home, immediately
calling Papa.

"He didn't look good," she informs Papa. "He was
only wearing underwear."

"What?" Papa boils. "Why?"

"All the political prisoners are being punished.
Fidel wants them to wear the same uniforms as common
criminals. All political prisoners are refusing, so the guards
confiscated their clothes."

"This is outrageous and inhumane!"

"I know. I couldn't believe it. Cristian looked
worn down. Does he always look that way?"

"Not when I've seen him. I was afraid something
was going on. Thank you, my friend, for making the trip
and giving me this information."

Several months go by, and political prisoners are
being disciplined again and will not be receiving visits,
letters, bags, or checks until further notice.

35 – Discovery

1969

It is 1969. Six long years have gone by since Cristian's arrest, when the regime relocates him to Guanajay, and the family receives word that visits can resume. Papa takes Alberto this time.

Inside, Papa and Alberto sit, waiting for Cristian. He arrives, giving his father and brother a big smile. Cristian walks up to the concrete half wall, separating him from his family. They lean over to hug each other.

Cristian sits down, alarming Papa by the figure before him. It has been two years since they have seen him. His tall, strong son now slouches as he looks at Papa with circles under his eyes. Cristian brushes his messy hair with his fingers as he puts on a smile for his family. Papa fills him in on the family while Cristian elusively answers questions, to spare Papa from worries.

"Cristian, have you noticed a lump in your throat?" Alberto asks.

"No," Cristian responds curiously. "What do you mean?"

"I see it when you swallow," he comments.

He feels around his throat, sensing what Alberto sees. "I haven't noticed it."

Papa and Alberto look at each other. "That doesn't seem right. Can you get it looked at?" Papa asks.

"I'll take a trip to the infirmary later," Cristian responds.

"You better and let me know what they say," Papa commands.

"Yes, Papa," Cristian forces a small smile.

After their visit, he goes to the bathroom to check out Alberto's observation. He requests to see the doctor, which triggers another move.

A week later, they transport Cristian to El Castillo del Principe, where they immediately escort him to the cell of another political prisoner. The prisoner, a physician, examines Cristian, discovering a cyst that needs to come out. The doctor informs the warden, and they begin preparations for an operation.

Weeks later, a surgeon removes the lump successfully and sends it out for a biopsy. The surgeon contacts Cecilia, under the impression that she is Cristian's wife, to inform her that the tumor is cancerous. Cuban's believe in sparing the patient from malignant diagnoses, fearing that knowledge would keep them from recovering.

Doctors give a cancer diagnosis to the immediate family, not the patient.

Cecilia takes a trip to the justice office to petition for his release, based on his illness. Restlessly she waits for a glimmer of hope.

36 - The Gate

1969

A month later, the prisoners make their usual trek to the dining hall to consume their bland meal. As Cristian lines up, a guard stops him.

"Come with me! The warden wants to see you," the guard commands.

"Why?" he questions.

"Go!" another guard shouts.

He follows the guard down the corridor. Many thoughts bounce around in his head: *Are they moving him again? Did something happen to a family member? Is he going to be interrogated again?*

He walks in spotting the warden at his desk reading over a document.

"Sit!" he commands. Cristian anxiously takes a seat. "You're being released today, under these conditions. You will report to the police station every month to confirm your location. Do you agree?"

"Yes," Cristian responds.

"The guard will take you to your cell right now. You will gather your things quickly and quietly. Is that understood?" he scolds.

"Yes, but what changed with my sentence?" he asks.

"That's all I know, now go," he waves to the guard.

"Take him to his cell, make sure he is packed and released quickly," he instructs the guard.

"Yes sir!" The guard salutes the warden, pulls Cristian up by his arm, and pushes him out the door.

Six years have passed since the government condemned Cristian to 12 years in prison. *What just happened?* He wonders but will not dwell on it right now. He gathers his things quickly to get out before they change their minds. He is holding his breath, hoping it's not another cruel trick of the government. Not being allowed to say goodbye to his friends bothers him. When he returns home, he will find a way to contact them.

The gate doors open. Cristian steps outside and his lungs fill with life as he takes a deep breath. In the sky, the bright sun fills him with vigor. Cristian takes his steps as a free man, rejoicing as he catches the leaves of the palm trees swaying softly in the wind. While he strolls down the street, the song of el Toti grows louder. He spots a café with a few customers and stops in for a mouthwatering café. *How he has missed that aroma and rich taste.* Free at last! Scouting the establishment, he spots a payphone. He takes out change to make his first phone call as a free man.

"I'm out!" Cristian tells Cecilia.

"That's great!" Cecilia rejoices. "We'll help you get settled." She hangs up the phone and prays to the heavens. Her trip to the justice office a month ago paid off.

With a brilliant smile on his face, he walks tall for several blocks to his destination. Cecilia and Maria pace up and down the sidewalk as they wait for him. Cecilia wears a new green dress. She fidgets with her handkerchief anxiously waiting. They will not let him out of their sight until he is safe. The next morning they take Cristian to his friend's house, then head to the communication company where he sends a telegram.

Papa, I'm coming home!
Love, your son Cristian

Afterword

Cristian undergoes three more surgeries and eventually has his thyroid removed. Cancer free, he survives the multiple operations with Cecilia by his side. Their relationship blossomed into a devoted love, and their marriage blessed them with three girls. He continued his pursuit for freedom and was eventually permitted to migrate to the United States.

Today, in Cuba, civilians continue to be incarcerated if they dare to protest over food shortages, necessities, or civil rights. Cubans are not allowed any public rallies that express disagreement with the regime. Those incarcerated continue to be tortured or disappear. Some of the civilians put through tortures do not survive.

In Loving Memory

The book was written in honor of Luis Carlos Sanchez and Jose Sanchez, who fought to liberate their country and restore the liberties that were taken from their fellow citizens.

Author Contact Information

Website: Lucygirolamo.com

Email: Lucygirolamo@gmail.com

Instagram: Lucy.Girolamo

Facebook: Lucy Girolamo, Author

References

Gonzalez, H. (2010). *Mi Lucha por la Libertad Recuerdos de Una Epoca Heroica.* United States: Hiram Gonzalez.

Rodriguez, C. S. (2011). *Cuba Cartas de Un Emigrante (1906-1980).* Spain: Publicaciones Digitales, S.A.

Made in the USA
Coppell, TX
26 August 2021